Roan: a fur coloring common in cats, dogs, and horses that does not "gray out" over time.

Saratoga Roan

Bree M. Lewandowski

Published by Bree M. Lewandowski, 2021.

SARATOGA ROAN

First edition. September 4, 2021.

Copyright © 2021 Bree M. Lewandowski.

ISBN: 979-8201623999

Written by Bree M. Lewandowski.

CHAPTER ONE

"Sure thing, Mr. Donne. Yep, I'll be sure to tell him. Alright. Yes, I understand. Alright then, you have a good day."

Matt hung up the phone.

"What's he want now?

"Says he came through last week. Wanted to check over Dusty, seeing as how the temperature was supposed to plummet."

It does that in Wyoming.

Rhett looked up from the computer screen. "And?"

"Apparently, rugging an Appaloosa will make them founder."

"You're kidding."

Matt shook his head. "Nope, from the almanac of equine knowledge himself."

"Some people shouldn't own horses. When do you think he'll decide that the pasture is bad for his horse too?"

"Probably around next month's payment."

Looking back to the computer; spreadsheets of numbers representing feed, hay, topicals, ointments, bedding, farrier fees, veterinarian fees, specialty supplements, custom order vitamins, and grooming gear, Rhett groaned.

"Probably. Anything else before I go check on the hires?"

"New client left a message."

"The one from New York?"

Matt nodded. "Says she'll be in town soon and wanted a walkthrough of the stables from Mr. Farris himself."

"Not happening. I got," he waved one hand towards the door of his office, "too much going on this week to sell some East-coaster on Saratoga Ranch. Discount her boarding fee."

"She paid in full two weeks ago."

"Then credit the account."

Matt grinned. "Don't you want to walk the nice, little lady from the Big Apple around?"

"Not in the least."

"I'll call back and let her know, boss man."

"Call the clinic, too, and see when the vet is coming to float teeth. He canceled on me last week. Half the stalls are overdue."

Matt mocked a salute and exited. Rhett looked at the laptop screen again, squinted at the march of numbers, and then stood, stretching his arms over his head.

Walk the new client through the ranch. She must think she's Lady Godiva, asking for a tour. She did pay up front, though.

Another week, another month altogether, and he might have accommodated her. Not today, though. Not ten days from now, either. Too much shit going on.

If he let himself dwell on it, he'd feel heat rise over the back of his neck, reach around to his throat and burn the nastiest words before they escaped his lips and choked him on his own emotions.

God had a sense of humor.

Rhett shut the computer and left his office. August winds, rolling through the stables, reached him, so did hay, feed, the sound of water splashing into troughs, and shovels pushing against ground cover, hefting out the previous night's muck. Ripe smells, especially in the late summer warmth.

Over-sized fans churned lazily from the open beam structured ceiling. However, their purpose was to keep air circulating for the horses overnight when the gates were shut, not cool the space. Among seasonal hired hands, there were always a few who couldn't take the offset, sweet scent and dropped off by the second week. Those who stayed either loved the animals enough to have that sense adjust or desperately needed a job.

Mid-morning, all the stable doors were swung wide. Some had already been mucked out but needed fresh bedding. Others were still packed down and lacked a body getting to it. With a capacity for thirty, twenty-four horses were tenants of Saratoga Ranch and their stalls had to be refreshed every day. This summer's batch of high schoolers were green and hadn't developed a concise method for accomplishing this chore. Of course, upon hiring, Rhett could have given them a routine order to follow. Been specific about how he wanted things done.

When the ranch belonged to his father, things were done *his* way and every hired hand knew it or was soon acutely informed. However, that system had been one of the many things to change because, really, the only thing that mattered was when the horses came in their bedding was clean and the food was fresh.

One of the girls, a late hire after one of the boys decided his delicate hands couldn't heft hay bales off the four-wheeler, accomplished the end goal each day, but struggled against herself.

Walking down the length of the stable, taking mental note of latches, beams, troughs, and any misplaced tack, Rhett saw her struggling.

"Jenny!"

She turned, flushed and sweating gaping circles from under her arms.

"Yes, Mr. Farris?"

"Use your legs, okay? Your mom called twice yesterday asking if you'd fainted, yet."

She blanched, white blotches pushing aside the red. "What'd you tell her?"

"I told her you're putting these boys to shame."

She looked down and smiled.

Typically, Wyoming's wind and weather braided strong bodies, but Jenny had been exempted. Allergies, asthma, and a frame like a willow branch made loving horses hard on her. Mrs. Jenny's mom tried to tell Rhett to let her daughter down gently after the first interview, hovering like a horse fly. Of course, she would never deny her daughter the chance to apply for a job she'd dreamed of having since she was in diapers, but, *of course,* he also understood a girl like Jenny wasn't built for ranch life.

He had disagreed; she'd never be built for it if she didn't have the chance.

"Legs," he repeated. "Okay?"

She widened her stance. "Yes, Mr. Farris."

"Go find Matt when you're done and ask him who gets brushed today."

She nodded then bent to her task.

It should always be like this. Hardworking people pushing themselves for these animals who asked for nothing but the space to be.

He labored to make this ranch exactly that. Five years now. Focus and effort. Construction on the stables, hacking the "barn and spittoon" look in favor of whitewashed walls, cobbled floors, and thick, wooden pens. Rental prices went up and he expanded the property lines and raised fences around fifteen acres. Horses boarding at his ranch would have room to roam and graze.

It was a business made of living bodies who deserved the best, if based only on that.

Murphy bumped into his leg. Among the barn cats, Rhett didn't have a favorite. However, Murphy and his bobbed tail slept at the house every night.

"You eat already, bud?"

The answering meow sounded like he'd swallowed a loogie once and never coughed it back up.

"Gonna come with me to unload the hay?"

"*Mrawl.*"

"Let's go, then. I could use some lifting."

Today's delivery was a half-ton load. The delivery company Rhett favored left the bed of the truck on half-ton days. The off-loading of multiple one-thousand pound bales was really a job for more than one person, but the heat lingering at the base of his neck was best relieved by manual labor.

Shirt sleeves rolled to his elbows, he unbuttoned the first few buttons for ease and range of movement. Murphy hopped lightly towards the top-most bale, drenching his gray coat in the Wyoming sun.

For a moment, Rhett tipped his face towards the light. Giant stacks of hay, their smell delicately sweet, surrounded him. The wind rushed and ruffled his hair.

Things were changing today, but what mattered wasn't. He needed to remember that. The work, the land, and the animals were there and unchanged, whether or not he pouted and licked old wounds like a stubborn mare.

Back shoved up against the first bale, his feet planted on the backboard of the trailer, Rhett thrust his body's weight backwards, getting the bale to tip, and allowing gravity to do the rest. With a dull heavy thud, it toppled down to the ground, strands of the pale green fodder breaking free and tumbling away.

Once it was all off-loaded, he or Matt would come back with a forklift and stack it on the ranch's four-wheelers to be properly stored. In fact, he only needed to get the highest bales off and could leave the rest for the machine, except he wanted to keep shoving his body at something. It cleared his head.

During high school, wrestling and football probably would have been good avenues.

Pity, he thought, ramming into another bale, *that I didn't know it then.*

Warm wind, never truly hot no matter the sun's rays, barreled and rolled. Its voice hushed and hummed, an ever-constant moan of enjoyment. It played on the fields, raced the horses, tumbling down and around the rocky landscape.

The wind caught and tugged Rhett's shirt when he took it off, forcing him to tie it around his waist before the wind made him monkey-in-the-middle of a game he'd never win. Warm air layered with grass, alfalfa, grain feed, scat, and dirt sounding like horses, stable hands, and life.

It wasn't changing.

If he could get it through his thick head. With a grunt, he slammed into another bale and turned his shoulder into the impossibly dense block. He'd weathered worse. Groaning, he managed it off the edge.

Murphy meowed and bounded down, off the truck bed.

"Be more of a man," came a familiar shout.

Rhett saw his older brother, dressed like he hadn't grown up in the same place he had, wearing slacks and a polo shirt.

"Let's see," Rhett started, ramming his first finger to his forehead in a mock attempt at recall. "If I'm not a man, then what am I?"

Tom shrugged. "I never knew the answer, either." He put his hands on the truck bed and pushed himself up. "Let me help you."

"And throw your back out? I'm not dealing with Dad alone. Get down."

"Make me."

Rhett pushed at him. "Be more of a saint."

"Be less of a martyr."

"Nougat," Rhett said, indicating which bale was next.

"Dummy," Tom answered, mocking the overly sullen tone his younger brother used.

Briefly, they worked in silence. They could have done it blind, sleep-deprived, and sicker than shit. Any day, any way.

Before Tom graduated high school, the ranch ran on two brothers and their father. Both boys were up at sunrise to get in what chores they could and back in the stables after they got off the bus. Working beside someone who knows exactly what needs to come next and knows exactly what the person next to them is one step away from is better synchronicity than a machine. People in tandem, unspoken and understanding.

When Tom graduated high school he took a partial scholarship at Wyoming Catholic College, and more hands were hired at the ranch. When Tom did not return to Saratoga after college, Rhett took on a managerial role while his father's drinking habit worsened.

Noticing the color on Tom's cheeks waning, Rhett sat down on one of the bales yet to be knocked off. Patting his knee for Murphy to come over, he asked how the trip had been. It was time enough for Tom to grab his inhaler if he didn't insist on being an idiot.

"The drive was rough. Dad doesn't..."

"I know."

"Doctor Jaye prescribed a sedative." He sat down, tapped at the gray knob of a tail, and gave the slim cat a thorough neck scratching. "It didn't agree with his stomach, though. We had to make a lot of stops." Tom untucked his shirt.

"Out the front or back?"

"Back."

"Can he still...?"

"When he's lucid."

"Which he wasn't on the drive."

"Not exactly."

Rubbing the back of his neck, Rhett stood. "Don't start. I signed up for this."

"I was only too happy to let you."

"Well, now you can be happy Dad's back."

Donning his shirt again, Rhett said he needed to get the forklift and load the hay bales. Tom clapped his brother on the shoulder and took out his inhaler, asking if he could use the Jeep and drive back to the house. He'd walked up to the barn, forgetting what Saratoga sun felt like in August.

CHAPTER TWO

Later in the day, Rhett sent the stable hands home. Before five o'clock, he told Matt to take an early evening. Calling the horses in from the pasture did not require more than one set of hands. Brushing down coats due for the task would only add to the amount of time he'd need to remain.

It wasn't cowardice. It was avoidance.

About six months ago, the fixtures of Tom's life came apart. The woman who had slept by his side for seven years took a long weekend which ended in a short email; their life together was no longer enough for her. Only days prior, his off-site job had downsized.

Rhett remembered the phone call, envisioning his sibling slumped over a kitchen chair, chin to his chest, soul dropped to his feet. Of course, he offered Tom live with him. However, Tom's silence served as the answer until Tom mentioned their father had been having dexterity issues. Not all the time, but frequently enough. He complained about it whenever he called, though it was the first Rhett had heard.

Then again, Rhett rarely received phone calls from *Father*.

Turned out, the gated community their father lived in did not pay distinct attention to who came and went. Also, it turned out the sudden fumbling and trembling was an indicator of Alzheimer's. Tom went from heartbroken and jobless, to living with his father, and then suddenly becoming lawful caretaker.

Until six months ago when the community failed to pass a state inspection and foreclosed.

On that phone call, early one blustering morning, his barn coat fully buttoned, Rhett said it was ridiculous for Tom and their father to live anywhere but the ranch, he'd redo the first floor and finish the basement.

When his older brother tried to argue, Rhett remembered tucking the cell phone into his shoulder and yanking on leather gloves. Wyoming's wind had taken down part of the small, enclosed pasture's fencing. Used to schedule, the horses did not understand why they had yet to be turned out and vocalized their displeasure. From harsh temperatures the night before, the metal fence was bitterly cold and siphoned dexterity from Rhett's hands through the gloves. Tom was going on about how they would find some other place to live. Dad's insurance was enough to keep them afloat for a while. Rhett didn't need to do this. Horses nudging stall doors, a nasty wind, and learning not only had part of the fence fallen but been tampered with, Rhett's words were sharp.

Just come! He'd have everything ready.

At his tone, Tom steeled, and for a few moments, they teetered on argument. He had thoughts about the offer. Rhett to the rescue again, huh? He should admit he didn't think his older brother had the stones to make it on his own. Let Strong Man Rhett swoop in. Tom didn't want to give him the satisfaction.

Rhett's counter had been nasty. Tom never had the sense to take care of himself; somebody better be there to pick him up and since Liz had shirked the duty, Rhett was stepping in.

The fence tottered. Wrangled wire punctured the gloves and Tom hung up. It was days before they spoke again, Rhett apologizing, and his brother owning he needed help.

ALL THAT WAS SIX MONTHS ago. The basement was finished. Walls had been knocked down to give his father's first floor room more of an apartment feel. A set of steps leading down into Tom's basement abode had been marked by handrails. The illness creeping upon Mr. Farris Senior made stairs a risk and should he want his caretaker, then taking risks was reckless.

Up on the second floor, more walls had come down and been reconstructed, turning what had been four bedrooms and a bath and a half into a one large living space. Not because he'd need to avoid his father, but because he'd need to get away.

In the barn, making short strokes from a stiff-wired brush into the dense fur of the ranch's lone donkey tenant, Rhett's groan did not rise above the repeating *reshow, reshow, reshow* sound of the bristles. Things would be different now. He wasn't an eight-year-old boy confused by his father's sharp comments. Adolescence had gone, leaving him far from the years where he puffed his chest and punched holes in walls.

Thirty now, he could let the man his father was bounce off him. Yet, what made him grip the wooden handle of the brush harder was knowing how fast the little boy in him could come out and how quickly fifteen year old him wanted to knock his father back on the ass.

Tom said they were too similar. Two big presences in the room, each trying to cancel the other out. Rhett believed his father never understood how his younger son wasn't just like him, even though Tom was excused from needing to be a carbon copy which goaded him all the more.

Maybe if their mother had been around more.

Or at all.

Raking the brush through the mossy, gray-brown fur once more, he patted Moses on the rump and then fished a small handful of alfalfa from his back pocket. Round brown eyes opened very wide at the unexpected treat.

"Enjoy. At least someone should enjoy their night tonight."

Overnight, the ceiling fans would continue to churn slowly. Walking the length of the barn, Rhett glanced in each stall. Fresh bedding for all. Ample food and water. A barn cat or two nestled in a far corner. Murphy slept in Rhett's office most nights. Rhett kept the door cracked for his convenience. In the tack room, a locker had been cleared for the new horse from New York.

There were contended snorts and munching. The heavy clonk of a horse kneeling down to flop over and sleep. The wind outside blew night over the land. Pushing down the main switch, all lights, save for emergency bulbs, cut out. Behind himself, Rhett pulled the heavy double doors.

Above him, a stretched and pulled indigo sky dwarfed the Wyoming land. This was Big Sky country. The night's breeze pushed the grass like ocean waves. It was a good night to walk back to the house.

"YA MISSED DINNER."

Hanging his keys on one of several hooks by the front door, Rhett nodded and rubbed the back of his neck.

Good to see you, too, Dad.

"Horses," he called to the voice hollering at him from another room.

"Something wrong with one of 'em?"

"Just an ass needing his rump brushed."

Callum Farris did not look away from the television. Sprawled on the reclining chair in his newly furnished room, he still looked very much the man Rhett had always known. When he learned about his father's diagnosis, he'd imagined a suddenly frail seventy-year-old. Outwardly, though, his father remained a man of John Waynes ilk. Tall and top heavy. Long legs and arms. Formidable and proud of it.

"Sorry I wasn't here when you got in."

Callum waved his hand. "Horses come first. I always told you that."

"You got everything you need in here? Everything okay?"

"Tom said you remodeled the house."

"If you need something—"

"Tom's here."

"Right. Well, I'm gonna—"

"Go eat. It's still on the stove."

"Sure. Good night."

Another hand wave.

In the kitchen, Tom sat hunched over a tablet. Rhett saw him glance up and quickly look down again. There was chili, he said. Should still be warm. He'd made it just the way Rhett liked: not spicy.

In lieu of thanks, Rhett made a comment about the number of eyes his brother currently had and said he needed something strong before he ate. Something strong enough to settle his stomach.

"He asked about you the second we got in."

"I bet he did."

"I can't babysit the both of you."

Rhett pulled a canister of ground chicory from the pantry. "No need. I can handle myself."

"If your back gets any straighter, you're gonna snap and you haven't spent more than ten minutes in the house with him."

Rhett filled the carafe of an electric kettle and set it to boil before pulling a kitchen chair the wrong way 'round, straddling it.

"Tom, I'm gonna be fine. I don't need to be on your radar, and you don't have to play referee between me and Dad. I'll behave."

"I'll ladle the next batch of chili with anchos if you don't."

"Then we'll all suffer."

Mounds of bubbles rippling inside the glass pot, its timid alarm beeped boiling level and Rhett pulled it from the heating mound. Scooping earthy dark grounds into a small, round strainer and snapping it shut, he poured the water over and left the strainer in a thick ceramic cup to steep.

Tom took his glasses off and said the new job would start next week. If anything needed doing around the house or stable, he could help. With affection, Rhett told his brother where he could shove it and scooped chili into a shallow bowl before taking the steaming mug and going upstairs.

SLUMBER BRINGS SOUNDS the sleeper may only be dimly aware of. In cities, it's the endless patter and murmur of cars, trains, and voices in a place where midnight means little more than one hour into a new day. Small towns bring small sounds. A dog's bark. A car droning by. Far overhead, the rumble of an airplane. Summer nights at a lake house play an incandescent chorus of crickets, water lapping on a mossy shore, and the infrequent call of an owl.

On Saratoga Ranch, it was wind. Rushing past his bedroom window, begging he listen to the tale of its travels that day. In an old house, despite the remodel, wood settled. pipes belched, and the wind played rapscallion on the roof.

Through all the harmony, he awakened to the sound of sobbing.

Rich, blue night sky, illuminated by a creamy, white waxing moon, spilled in through the large windows of his bedroom, soaking the rumpled quilt he lay under. He sat forward. Downstairs, someone wept. Rhett felt his heart's beat quicken.

He knew this voice, distorted though it was, and swept the blanket off. Over the course of Tom's taking care of Callum, he'd explained a lot. Some days lucidity evaporated, replaced by confusion and alarm. There was no trigger. There was no way to guess an episode's duration. Sometimes the disillusioning fog rolled in frequently, but then there were weeks where Callum showed no signs of the condition lurking within his mind.

Rubbing the back of his neck, Rhett went downstairs.

Outlined in the dimness was a big man, slumped over himself, flapping his hands against his legs, sniffing, and coughing on his own sobs.

Compacted emotions formed over the years jammed in Rhett's throat, hot and jagged. What was supposed to be words came out as a strangled grunt.

Callum turned.

'"Can you help me?"

Confusion, innocent and bewildered, took away years from his father's face though not the signs of age. Simultaneously, he was seven and seventy.

Rhett cleared his throat. "What's wrong?"

The big hands flapped again. "I want another blanket, but I don't know where they are."

Tom had described this and how alien it was. These linked up moments where big man Callum became the child he might never have been, himself. The sight rang with a Biblical, clarion tone. Everything in its season, turn, turn, turn.

Tom said the first time it happened, he had to look away, while he yanked his emotions back in order. It had been something about a sandwich. They were in a restaurant and Callum had taken off the top piece of bread to squirt ketchup on the turkey shavings. He'd frozen, bottle in hand, suddenly weeping over how there was too much turkey.

Moving between the night's indigo shadows, Rhett clenched his jaw.

"I'll get you another blanket."

"Thank you. My face is wet."

"I'll..." Rhett coughed. "I'll get you a towel, too."

With a folded blanket in the hand he refused to acknowledge was shaking, he went to the linen closet next and pulled out a small towel.

Emotion screamed to break free from his subconscious. Memories surged to capture the forefront of his thoughts. Pull a calf from a birthing mare, rein in a spooked gelding, load hay bales manually when the forklift was broken—Rhett considered himself a strong man.

Apparently, Tom was stronger, and he wouldn't forget it now that his lungs strained to burst.

Placing the blanket on Callum's lap, he handed his father the towel. However, the big man did not appear to see either item and stared out the window.

"The sky is pretty tonight."

"Yep."

"I should go to sleep, or I'll be tired in the morning."

Where was a third of this man who spoke so simply when Rhett was eleven and toppled off his mount? Palms and knees stinging, red in the face, to think he could have met this placid father and not the one who glanced at him and walked away.

Rhett patted the blanket and placed the towel on top of it. "Well, here you go."

Callum looked up at him. "Will you help me?"

"Help you...?"

He mimicked his son, patting the blanket and then the towel.

Burning warmth blurred Rhett's vision. Unable to speak, he nodded to his father's request and unfolded the plain green quilt, shaking it out so it hovered for an instant in the air and then floated down. Then, one hand clenched so tightly he might snap his knuckles, Rhett took the soft square towel and wiped under his father's eyes and nose.

Happily, Callum smoothed the blanket over himself. "You're a nice young man."

"Th-thanks."

"I'm tired now." Callum wriggled under the covers. "Good night."

Striding as if suffocated for breathable air, Rhett walked from the room. "G'night, Dad."

SLEEP LEFT HIM RESTLESS, plagued by memories best forgotten.

Two voicemails ten minutes before morning chores started informed Rhett two of the strapping high school boys hired on for the summer were not coming for reasons not specifically specified. Normally, Rhett would have shrugged it off, but the new tenant arrived today and the company transporting the horse had not developed a good reputation for knowing what they were doing, despite their charges.

Additionally, one of his pickiest clients was scheduled to load their horse for a showing competition. Any day Ms. Henries bestowed the charm of her presence on the ranch was a day Rhett would have preferred to be behind his desk, behind a shut door.

At the stables, checking to see if any other surprise messages came in, Rhett snapped at Matt, informing him of things they both already knew.

Get the horses in the pasture. Remember five of them are in the smaller paddock The boys aren't coming, and Jenny only works so fast. That damned new horse is coming and space in the tack room has got to be cleared out, even though the locker was ready.

The owner had been generous in her payment, but she might be expecting Mozart and ceramic water troughs. East coast riders had expectations. By the time she got here, Rhett would be lucky if his shirt wasn't thoroughly soaked and hay particulates poking out of his eyelashes.

Horses were turned out one at a time. Not everyone got along. A few of the mares bristled over one another. More than a few geldings played alpha. And some, though eager to get out of their stables, loitered in the long hall, sniffing every last thing.

"Motion, Mia, Quin, Holly, and Will, right?"

"Yeah. Get a muzzle on Mia today. She's been snippy with Holly lately. We'll bring her in first later so she can eat longer."

"Yes, boss man."

Matt hollered at Mia, asking if she was ready to start her day and Rhett walked to the far end of the stable, towards the last two stalls. Big snouts lolled over the gate, nudging to be rubbed. His big boys. Slaughterhouse rescues.

Some people shouldn't own horses. A stunning Soviet Draft bay, Ben had a growth on his eye thought to be cancerous, though he still had years of good riding in him. A chestnut Ardennais, Sam's pastern injury had not healed correctly, and it was assumed he was useless. A veterinarian confirmed Ben's growth benign, and all Sam needed was physical therapy. Both would live out their years in comfort here, Sam in full retirement and Ben for light ranch horse duty.

The black snout and red clay colored snout nudged his shoulders in turn.

"Good morning, boys. I'm letting you two out first today. Give the others someone to follow. We're busy."

Ben snorted.

"You're not working today, bud. Keep Sam company."

Unlatching both gates, he let the massive bodies move forward, giving each rump a pat to keep them from lingering beside him like overgrown dogs.

"Rhett!"

"What?"

"That transport company called. They'll be here in an hour."

Pushing the stable doors shut, with a quick glance to ensure both his boys kept moving, Rhett groaned and took a muzzled Mia by the lead.

"I'm surprised they even called ahead."

"They said an hour, tops."

"Great. When Jenny gets here have her clear out space in the tack room."

Matt moved to the next stall and nodded before opening the gate while Rhett hoisted a shovel from its hook and grabbed a wheelbarrow to take on possibly the most important task of each morning—mucking.

CHAPTER THREE

Wheelbarrow filled with soiled bedding it was dumped into a large trough attached to an ATV. An average of three stables could be swept clean before needing to dump the discard. Over the years, neighbors said Saratoga Ranch could have a beautiful crop of something, if they chose. Nothing like horse manure for gardening. Several local farmers who came regularly in the warm months to get a load of ranch fertilizer, swearing their vegetables tasted different without it.

The air smelled different without it, too. Urine and scat, soaked into the bedding, when pulled apart with a tonged shovel, blossomed into a rare, high smell that clung to a person. Lodged itself right at the topmost point of the nose and refused to be blown clean.

Younger, Rhett used to get a kick out of relatives' visits. His cousins were always so excited to see and pet the horses. Like a pied piper, he'd lead them into the middle of the barn and stop, waiting for the looks on their faces to change. Eyelids would pull back, squint, and then fill with tears. Then one nostril would lift unnaturally high, followed by the other, squelching their faces like over-ripe persimmons.

Sometimes, he pretended he had no idea what they smelled. Other times, he said if they wanted to spend time around horses, they needed to toughen up.

Every now and again, when teens came looking for a job, especially if they admitted to not having worked around a ranch before, the infantile side of him got a kick watching their expressions pucker when he gave them the tour.

Hefting another shovel into the wheelbarrow, he admitted it might have been nice if the barn had not been built to dissuade the wind from blowing through, toying with gear and gates, frightening the horses. Summer sat heavy today.

Rhett stood the shovel upright and drew his forearm across his brow. He gave Matt crap for wearing a bandanna during barn chores, but then Matt rarely dealt with sweat stinging his eyes. Of course, though, sweat didn't bother *real* men. And real men didn't take their shirts off when they got hot. Work was work.

That lesson had come with a sharp smack across the back one oppressive September day. He'd been fifteen and bare chested. Callum had a pair of stirrups in his hand when he passed behind. It wasn't so much that the swipe hurt, but that it was unexpected. Rhett remembered falling forward, his jeans instantly soaked with horse piss. Adolescent testosterone had surged and he'd whipped around on his father. The challenge he felt swell his chest and burn his eyes was met with imperial immobility.

The gentle man in the moon's glow last night would have cowered. The bent back and helpless hands could not comprehend such malevolence.

Pushing the wheelbarrow in front of the next stall, Rhett wondered if the man he knew as his father and the one he met last night were the same person. In the cavern that was his father's chest, did a mellow man exist? Or was it only an illusion of dementia?

He didn't know and didn't want to.

Hay and shavings scattered as he dumped another scoop into the wheelbarrow.

Over the sound of his thoughts, Jenny hollered, saying she was done organizing a spot in the tack room.

"Grab a shovel, then!"

THROUGH BILIOUS CLOUDS, the sun pushed higher in the sky and the morning moved on.

Most phone calls were left to voicemail, except when a solid five minutes of incessant ringing passed, and Rhett practically threw his shovel down to yank the phone from its charging port. One of those calls had been the vet's office. The doctor wasn't able to make it today. They apologized. Tomorrow, he'd be there. How many horses needed their teeth floated again? Apparently, his schedule was solidly packed.

So was the wheelbarrow of shit Rhett pushed in front of himself.

Before eleven o'clock, glimpsing how red Jenny's cheeks and neck were getting, he told her to take lunch and then write down all the messages from the answering machine. She had smoothed hair back from her face and nodded. Assuring himself she wouldn't try and sneak back and finish the stall she'd been working on, Rhett fetched clean bedding and spread it out.

Glancing to see where Matt was in the march of stalls, Wyoming's wind brought the sound of a diesel truck clamoring up the long drive.

It must be those idiots from the transport company. Did Ms. East Coast know she'd hired hacks to deliver her beloved pony across the nation? Or had she been impressed by their glitzy website?

Oh, he'd checked it out, after hearing the name and opinions from other stables. Polished website and oddly affordable prices. Yeah. Because they shambled around in a vehicle that would test even the most patient horse.

Rhett unbuttoned his shirt. Shrugging it off, he snapped it free of debris and then wiped his face before putting it back on, buttoning it halfway. With a holler to Matt, he walked out of the barn to meet the truck.

The trailer wasn't properly rigged. Rhett folded his arms across his chest. As the idiot driver slowed to figure out how to back the trailer towards the barn, Rhett made sure he was in the guy's line of sight. If he was gonna break anything on Saratoga Ranch, he'd have to break through the owner first.

From inside the trailer, Rhett heard the horse cry. A shrill whinny. Poor babe. How long had she been knocked around, bound for her "safety" and terrified?

"Hey!" he yelled, waving his arms over his head. "Cut the engine!"

The man behind the wheel looked baffled.

"Fucking cut the engine! I'll get the horse!"

"You sure, man? She's a smart bitch."

"Smarter than you, probably. Stay in the truck."

The small van rocked. Hooves beat against corrugated aluminum. Rhett started talking, his voice even and low. None of it needed to make sense. What this mare needed to hear was control and steadiness.

Outside of the world that knows them, horses are rarely portrayed as intuitive, sensitive animals, except they truly are. However, they're also overgrown dogs who don't know their own strength and rely on a pack leader.

She brayed, held still, and then stomped. Rhett kept talking.

Undoing the latch, he swung the door back slowly, but from inside she kicked. Within an instant, assuming her rump would be facing him and intending to come around her left side, there was a bolt of cream and honey markings.

Rhett jumped back and his heart bolted from his ribs.

He knew those markings. A backside and snout like she'd played in a honey pot. A painted palomino.

He *knew* this horse.

Five years ago, he cared for this horse and been in love with her rider.

"Succotash!"

He whistled and the mare turned. Her snout dropped low, and she trotted towards him. Hands shaking, he reached for her, memories he'd torn from his heart slicing anew.

A figure like damn. Dark red hair and pale blue eyes. Her voice was husky for a woman, one that blew his senses to smithereens when she was between his arms and all her words for his ears only. His plans had been to make her his wife. She didn't have time to wait for him, though, and walked.

Walk.

Ha.

Cassandra ran.

Pressing his forehead to Succotash, letting the mare nudge and bump affectionately, he tried to steady himself. So, the new tenant from New York, the one who wanted a walk-through of the stables from the owner, who paid well in advance...

Somehow it was just like her. Fucking brazen. So, she hadn't changed. Twenty-four now and still bucking.

I didn't try to break you. I didn't want to tame you, but you never let me show you what I did want. Impatient brat.

Succotash pushed Rhett off her nose.

"You done with my affections, too?" He patted her neck. "Come on, then."

Docile yet aware, she followed Rhett. Though she wore a bridle he did not need to guide her with it. Her owner, from day one, had done a bang-up job of training. An independent matched by an equal, Succotash's owner had made sure her horse was sound beyond question. Even on days when the natural tart nature of Tash's mare side came out, her lead's hand was understanding without being weak. A princess and a queen, each with heads high, respecting the other.

"No fucking way!"

Untying the bandanna from his head and using it to wipe his face and neck, Matt came out of a stall.

"I never thought I'd see this beauty again."

"Me neither. But you couldn't have told me the name on the account? Verlice isn't that common."

"She never called. It was an email one day with the horse's name and a deposit into the ranch's PayPal account. I didn't hardly look at the name."

"What about the request—"

"It wasn't her, Rhett. It was a guy who called." Matt looked at him. "I wouldn't do that to you."

"I know. I just..." He rubbed the back of his neck.

Matt nodded, patted Rhett on the shoulder, and told Succotash to behave before walking away.

JENNY GUSHED. EYES wide like a little girl seeing the toy of her dreams, she asked Rhett three dozen questions about Succotash. Though she was respectful of a horse who did not know her, Rhett knew she was dying to brush and pet the honey and cream coat. However, given that this was her first day on the ranch, Succotash would be largely left alone. New sounds, smells, horses, and faces after a long trek, she needed time to adjust.

Removing the ripped bridle, Rhett tossed it to Jenny, looking for any lacerations from Tash's struggle in the trailer.

"Do you want me to get anything for her, Mr. Farris?"

"Grab cinnamon oil from the tack room. We'll put it in her food tonight, too."

"In her food?"

"People use lavender to calm horses a lot, but cinnamon does the same and it can help settle stomach and bowel movements. She had a rough go this week and if I remember correctly, she gets constipated real easy."

Jenny grinned. "Nobody likes to be constipated."

"Damn uncomfortable."

Jenny lingered. "Do you think her owner will be around a lot?"

Probably. I seem to be raking up the luck in spades, lately.

"I don't know. Why?"

She looked down. "I'd like to brush her."

"I don't think Tash's rider will have a problem with that. She," he cleared his throat, "she started out here, a lot like you."

"She did?"

"She would have gotten the oil first, though," he answered, with a wink. "The horse come first."

Unhooking her elbows from over the gate, she sped off.

Not only would Cassandra have gotten the oil in an instant, she probably would've cried over how stressed her mount was and settled herself in a corner of the stall.

Sitting cross-legged, head tipped to one shoulder and asleep to the world was how he'd first met her.

Rhett long suspected that if Cassandra had been a boy, green as a suburban lawn, she never would have worked at Saratoga Ranch. However, the day she stood in front of his father was the same day one of the volunteers from a shelter forty miles down the road had called.

Shannon Barnes, twenty-five years in the business, housing cows and goats from an illegal breeding getup at the time, did not have an extra stall to take in an owner surrender. She had told Callum Farris she was loading up the painted mare herself and driving over. He needed to get a stall ready.

That painted mare turned Cassandra's head so fast his father was blinded by red hair and when she looked back at him, with wonder and hope in her eyes, the man of the West melted.

He made her a deal. He didn't have time to teach her every little thing she needed to know about equine care; however, he also did not have the time to train and break a three-year-old mare. If Cassandra came to the ranch every day, willing to work hard and learn fast, the horse was hers.

On a directive from Callum to find "the new girl," it had been late afternoon when Rhett first saw her, asleep in the corner of the stall. Her aunt had called, wondering how long her niece's first day of work could possibly be. Stopped in the middle of lugging feed bags from the truck to the silo, a job that had been imperative an hour prior, Rhett was irked to suddenly be a task rabbit.

Until he saw her and the side of himself that relished the wind's sound and a horse's physique moving through a canter to a gallop, saw a young Epona before him. Goddess of mares and foals in Celtic lore, she is untouchable upon horseback, her virginal beauty bared for all to see. Flanked in depictions by two horses, she is their caretaker and only those passed from the world of the living will know the presence of her company and the choice of her celibacy. Perhaps, before she assumed her place as caretaker of horses she lived as one of them, accepted nowhere else.

He didn't remember now what he said to wake her up. After seeing heavy lids reveal doll-like, round eyes of diluted sky blue, his insides clenched, and he could only motion for her to get up. Dusting straw from her jeans and shirt, unaware it also clung to her hair, hers had been the first real words.

He must be one of the Farris boys. Was he Tom or Rhett? Mr. Farris seemed to yell both those names a lot. Her name was Cassandra Verlice and she'd named this horse Succotash because Sophie didn't fit a filly like her.

It didn't fit, but he never thought her name suited her either.

Tash snorted.

"I don't need your opinion, Miss."

Eventually, Jenny returned.

Taking the small bottle, Rhett told her to watch how and where he applied the oil and if the horse still seemed unsettled come the morning, she could rub on a little more.

Dutifully, Jenny bobbed her head in ascent and Rhett stepped out of the stable, hardly latching the door behind himself when a figure at the corner of his eye stopped him.

Out of his heart and mind, he'd driven the memory of that silhouette. Still, with painful clarity, she stepped forward now. Backlit in the afternoon sun. Long hair, windswept. Worn tooled boots. High-waisted jean shorts and a shorn tee-shirt, off-set over one shoulder.

She was the same. So damned the same. Careless and carefree. Wild and determined. Five years ago, she bolted from Wyoming, leaving him pounding on her aunt's door at two in the morning, demanding to know where she had gone after he found his number blocked.

She comes sauntering in here now, like fucking nothing.

"I hope you're not mad."

On the stone floor, the boots echoed, tapping every fiber of his muscles. Aside from the motion of her body, everything before Rhett's eyes stilled while his instincts revolted at her approach. Yet, in the same instant, he could yank her into his arms. In the same moment, he could throw her to the ground.

To his silence or the twisted look he felt on his face, Cassandra kept talking.

"I had to bring Succotash to the best. I'm not trusting anyone else with her."

He didn't trust his voice to be even and wondered if he wanted to give her steady and controlled. She didn't deserve it. She deserved every emotion clawing at his insides. For such a bold woman, she'd been a coward back then. Must be nice to stroll back in here, repercussions of actions buried six feet deep.

"I didn't think I'd ever see this horse again."

Cassandra smiled. Plump lips. Never a shock of color on them. Chapstick, at most. That mouth had teased and adored him. He hated it now.

"You were her first man."

And who was yours, Cassandra? We both know it wasn't me.

"And she'll never have better."

Cassandra stopped and leaned against the stable, reaching out for Succotash but keeping her eyes on him.

"It's good to see you again, Rhett. Can I say you look good?"

"You can say whatever you want. I'm busy, though."

"Fine. I'm not trying to stop you."

No?! What the fuck are you doing here? You're telling me you up and decided to move all the way from New York state back to Wyoming after five years? You left whatever job you had, uprooted Tash, severed any professional ties you had to come back and start again? You were never a spiritual woman. Don't try and tell me you woke up one morning and decided your roots really were back here. I could have told you that! I did tell you that! This land is in you the same as it's in me. But nothing I said to you stuck. You did like you wanted. Then and now.

"You're not," he said, walking away.

CHAPTER FOUR

"**I**t's good to see you again, Rhett. Can I say you look good?"

It was true, whether she said it or not. Five years had sculpted him. Toned the lines of his face and hardened his shoulders and back. The softness of his arms she knew was gone, replaced by dense muscle. Even the blue-green of his eyes had solidified into hazel. At twenty-four she exactly hadn't left a boy, but this wasn't the same Rhett Farris she remembered.

"You can say whatever you want. I'm busy, though."

"Fine. I'm not trying to stop you."

"You're not."

He walked away and she watched him go, raking hair from down her back over one shoulder. He was still a pleasure, coming or going. But if he was going then her hair didn't need to be down while she brushed Succotash.

Snapping an elastic off her wrist, Cassandra wove a quick tight braid and tossed the now tamed locks back around. Besides, Tash enjoyed hair and horse spit is its own brand of goo.

Before getting inside the pen, she looked around at how Saratoga Ranch had changed, clearly more successful now than under Callum's hand. The John Ford look had been replaced by varnished exposed beams and cobbled floors. Latches on each of the stalls were brushed brass and even the pens themselves had been updated with thick, dark wood, sanded and stained.

Part of Cassandra wanted to come back and find patched gates and splintering wood. Part of her wanted to return and find the horses she remembered in their pens. And within a far corner of her chest, she wanted to find Rhett with overgrown hair across his forehead, sweating through threadbare tee-shirts. That version of him was part of the home she remembered, and it stung to come back and find the memory exactly that, a recollection.

Cassandra stepped in the stall. Pulling a worn brush from her back pocket, she drew it over Tash's coat. She'd had the brush so long, it wasn't serviceable anymore, but her girl loved the feel across her creamy honey-pot body. Normally, the sound brought its own comfort to Cassandra, but her thoughts snagged like stubborn tangles in a mane.

Aunt Louise had been wonderfully supportive and uncomfortably honest when she called a few weeks ago.

Her father's lone sister had died and left a house for Cassandra in the will. The executor said she could handle the whole thing between phone calls and emails, there was no need for her to leave New York. Initially, that had been Cassandra's plan. There was nothing for her in Wyoming, certainly not her father. And his sister had been little more than an acquaintance. She told the executor he could handle the whole thing and notify her when he needed a signature.

In fact, she'd gotten off the phone in a hurry because she had lessons to teach and her own training to attend later; although, sometimes training with Martin led to other things, off horse-back. By the time she arrived at Adirondack Stables, thoughts of an unseen house were as many miles from her mind as New York from Wyoming.

She'd taken an hour for lunch and then tacked up Succotash. Guiding her alternately between a walk, trot, and canter, Cassandra thought about trivial things. The bridle she special-ordered was late. A judge from a previous show suggested Tash's rider tuck her hair up under the helmet. Had she made plans with Martin for dinner? Had she left the bedroom window open?

A shot fired. Later, she'd learn it was someone's idiot brother who thought firing a (unsettlingly realistic) toy gun at the start of his sister's hurdle pattern would be funny.

Tash had been mid-rhythm, transitioning from canter to walk. The sound flattened her ears and she bucked, then reared like a rank rodeo stallion. Cassandra's grip on the reins was light, her seat lazy. Jostled forward and then thrown back, she tumbled backwards off the mare's rump. Braced for impact, swallowing a yelp, those petty ruminations evaporated before one name.

Rhett.

Falling, she wished Rhett was there to catch her, or his could be the hand she grabbed getting to her feet. All at once, she wished it was him taking Tash's reins and walking her around to settle her nerves.

In a wild heartbeat, she wanted Rhett and everything that came with him. Wyoming. Those almost endless skies. Wind and weather unpredictable. Sandy clay soil that lingers on boots and hands. Wide spaces where the horizon blended earth and sky.

She canceled the lesson. Told Martin she wasn't riding Tash after a scare like that, and she had barely started the car when she called the executor back. Catching his voicemail, she informed him she was buying a plane ticket tonight and making arrangements to see the house.

Aunt Louise had received her niece's news quietly. Of course, she told Cassandra, she was welcome, but enthusiasm did not gush from her tone. In fact, she quickly asked if something was wrong. From previous texts and emails, she thought Cassandra was doing well. What had changed?

There was no pretending with Louise. She'd always been painfully honest, and honesty was due her now.

"You're moving all the way back just for him?"

"Not entirely. I miss Wyoming."

"But if he wasn't here?"

"Well, he is. I already checked if the ranch is still running."

"Cassie. I'm not going to ask if you're sure about this. But I will say I don't think it's a good idea."

Keeping her strokes down Succotash's back steady and long, Cassandra hated to think, once again, Louise might be right. It's one thing to have a profound realization. It's completely different to uproot everything around that epiphany.

Tash bobbed her head.

Even if it wasn't a smart move on her part, she'd make the best of a dumb decision. The house could be a disaster; her things were in storage. It might take time to find an apartment. The money left in the will, plus her own savings, was cushion enough. She was back, back where she should have always been, and intended now to stay. Whether Rhett was part of her future or not.

Anger, hurt, desire, and shock had hardened his eyes and locked his jaw. Little doubt lingered in her mind a part of him still cared. The doubt came with whether he wanted her love again.

"Well, look what Sam Hill and tarnation brought back."

Cassandra didn't need to turn around.

"Did ya miss me, Matt?"

"I tell you what. I missed this horse," he said, reaching over the gate with an offering hand.

"Fair enough."

From out of the pen, she came, and he clapped her on the back. And although his tone and expression were friendly, he didn't return her smile.

"I tell you, when I saw your girl, I thought maybe I'd tied my bandanna too tight and cut the blood circulation around my head. Making me see things."

"We're both here."

"You sure are."

Retrieving a cookie from his pocket, he held it over the gate, pretending to have the greatest interest in Tash taking it.

"You don't sound too happy."

"Can't say I am." Succotash took the treat, and he produced another. "You left a mess."

"I know."

"You got balls coming back."

Well, someone's gotta have them, right? I didn't notice Rhett chasing me down. Not that I expected him to.

"I'm not here to undermine your masculinity, Matt."

Succotash was on her third munchie.

"What *are* you doing here?"

"My dad's sister died. Left me a—"

"Bullshit."

"Since when do I need to answer to you?"

"You never did to anyone else."

"Matt." She grabbed his arm.

Offering one final crunchy, he looked at her.

"I made a mistake."

"And if you weren't so selfish, you'd have left it made. He's got the business now. Tom and Callum are back underfoot in that house, and you prance in here, shaking your ass at him. Don't play dumb, I saw you, and think you can get your way?"

On the ride to the airport, during the flight, over and over again as she drove up the road to Saratoga Ranch, she told herself that whatever storm and thunder got thrown her way, she was going to take.

She had left him ugly. No break-up. No attempt to talk. Within hours of their fight, she sat on a plane. Right before takeoff, she had blocked Rhett's number. That had been it. She couldn't take his hot and cold anymore. A man doesn't kiss a woman, turn her body into flames, and then not take her to bed.

So, she took her sexual frustration and threw it back in his face. She wasn't enough to sleep with? Then she wasn't anything at all.

Except she was still the woman who loved him. However, proof of that wouldn't come with her merely walking into the stables.

"I want him back."

"He doesn't want you."

"I don't think that's true."

"He doesn't want more of what caring for you means."

"That's his decision."

"And if he makes the same decision a second time, then fucking respect it, Cass."

ON THE WAY BACK TO Louise's, the facilitator called. He was in the area, if she wanted to look at the house. At a protected left turn, Cassandra yanked a U-turn.

Located in Carbon County, Old Haymaker Place was a small town. A few friends from high school lived there, though they hadn't been dear enough for her to bother learning if they still resided there. And while her father's sister was still living, she certainly never visited.

Family did not mean the same thing to everyone.

Clearly.

Her mother cried unfit to handle motherhood. Even early memories included Louise and in one of those recollections, her mother left to run an errand and never came back. Eighteen months later brought an autopsy report, substance overdose. Her father had not come to the funeral, although he did call, asking if Cassandra needed anything.

Not from him.

Because the house was his father's sister's, taking it pricked her pride. She didn't need it to stay in Wyoming. For the next several months, money wasn't a problem. Even if she liked the place, nothing beheld her into keeping it. In fact, she didn't have to get further than the driveway if she didn't want to. The executor wouldn't care; his paycheck came regardless.

At the end of a "no-outlet" street, she pulled her rental car into a short gravel driveway. That would suck during winter, which could be practically nine months out of the year in Wyoming. In clear need of power-washing, the house matched its stubby driveway. Small windows faced the street, overlooking an overgrown lawn. From the little Cassandra knew of her aunt's last days, she had been in hospice care, so landscaping didn't rank much on the list of important things.

Greeting her on the small front stoop, the facilitator assured her there were affordable mowing services in the area, but she should be prepared for the interior to match. Apparently, things had gone downhill quickly for her aunt, and it had been a close friend from church who insisted and paid for hospice.

"Really?"

He nodded, unlocking the door. "I have her contact information, if you want it."

"So, she was the only one who...?"

"She and your aunt were very close. It was Lynn who notified next of kin after Sherie passed."

"My father, you mean."

"Yes, Ms. Verlice."

Lamps with mock Tiffany shades adorned a modest front room. Pictures, matching in theme only, painted the walls. Birds. All kinds of birds. And all paintings. No photographs. In a galley style kitchen, birds flew over the wallpaper and shelf lining. A large mural of seagulls was the sole décor in the main bedroom. Pigeons decorated the shower curtain in the bathroom and chickadees perched throughout a small second bedroom that looked like it had been used to store books about birds.

The furniture was all very plain, almost utilitarian. A kitchen table folded out from the wall. Cassandra did not see a television anywhere. However, a sizable stereo, unfashionably large from decades ago, stood where a TV might have been.

Quaint slides away from charm at a certain point. It loses its kitschy charisma on the way down when beloved becomes burdensome. A single chair in a narrow kitchen. Only still images on the walls. Colors lacking life. Slim beds with one pillow each. Not even a vase of artificial flowers.

"Did you meet Lynn?"

"Yes. She gave me her set of keys."

"Text me her number. If she wants anything before it gets cleared out."

"You intend on keeping the house?"

Such a quiet life had lived here. Her thoughts of Cassandra were wholly unknown to her niece, but without those thoughts, she wouldn't be back where she belonged. At the least, she owed it to Sherie to keep this house out of a stranger's hands.

"Yes. But all this needs to go."

"Everything?"

"Except the big painting in the bedroom and this one. Get some company to come and clear it out, but I want to get in touch with Lynn, first."

If it had been an era for heel clicking and bowing, she got the sense the Verlice executor would have done both. His nod of ascent was bedside manner perfect, brief and understanding.

By the time Cassandra got back in her silver sedan, Lynn Deen's contact information waited in her inbox.

NUMEROUS THOUGHTS MERGED in and out of her consciousness on the way out of Old Haymaker Place: Learning about a life unknown to her when she had been considered part of that person's life. Everything Matt said. The way Rhett looked.

So, Mr. Farris and Tom were back on the ranch. Funny. She never pictured them leaving. Well, maybe Tom. He didn't bleed horseflesh the way his father and brother did.

What made them come back? Had she just missed seeing Callum in the stables? Even from the first day working at Saratoga, he was a hard man to miss. Although she'd been intimidated by the perpetual scowl he wore, it only took a few weeks, in those early days, before she came to cherish his bushy, unkempt eyebrows and grimacing smile. It would be good to see him again.

Deciding to stop at a popular coffee shop chain, then deciding to pull through the drive-thru instead, Cassandra hoped little had changed about Rhett's father. If just one thing could be the same and match her heart for this place, she wouldn't feel so itchy in her own skin.

Coming back *was* the right decision. Being under these skies again confirmed that. Stepping out into the wind, watching it blow clouds and weather so the sky, from one moment to the next, never looked the same. And if all she got was the air and the ground, Succotash beside her, then that would be enough.

Though barely.

Making sure she placed the guest ticket on the dashboard after parking alongside the curb of the subdivision, Cassandra glanced at her phone's clock. Aunt Louise probably wouldn't be home yet, circulation desk hours at the library were no joke.

Might be nice to make dinner for Louise, like old times. If ingredients for baked spaghetti were to be had, then she knew exactly what would be on the menu tonight, extra nostalgia points if celery and beef broth were present for braising.

Despite having grown up in her aunt's care, Cassandra never did understand her love for celery.

Rummaging for the appropriate pasta pot, it would be like high school years again. A ready dinner and her aunt's mild smile. Would Aunt Louise ask about her day at the ranch, now as then? If she didn't, it would hover like a bloated blimp over dinner.

Any answer would be difficult.

Oh, the man she faked a one-night stand for? Just to get him angry enough so he would get over his old-fashioned notion of "deflowering" her? The man she adored and doubted? The same man she woke sweating over and then struck with all her strength one day when he pushed her hand away from the button on his jeans?

Him?

No. He hadn't been happy to see her and though she'd prepared herself for his reaction, it hurt.

AFTER THE CELERY WAS braised and the kitchen smelled like basil, tomato, and Thanksgiving, Cassandra filled Louise's plate, then a fluted wine glass with the sparkling cucumber water she enjoyed. Her aunt asked if she remembered the time Cassandra first attempted a meal like this.

"I do, thank you very much."

Louise grinned. "You looked so defeated."

With a full dinner plate, Cassandra sat down, trying not to laugh.

"You would be too, when the dough you made didn't rise the first time because the yeast was dead, so you try again but forgot the salt because you were upset about the yeast."

"It was the most delicious bland crust I've ever had."

Cassandra laughed and shook her head. "And I haven't tried to make dough since."

In pleasant quiet, touched only by the sound of forks tapping plates, both women ate. Cassandra knew her aunt enjoyed silence over dinner. Even the muted muttering of the library, six days a week, was enough to make her yearn for uninterrupted calm when she got home.

So, it was after Cassandra cleared the table, Louise spoke. "How did things go today?"

The question was gently asked.

"Seeing him again was..."

Wonderful.

"...but I don't know."

CHAPTER FIVE

"I can help around the house."

"Tom, you don't need to earn your keep," Rhett answered, pouring brewed chicory into a mug.

Early dawn's pale, pale yellow and powdered blue colored the morning sky in broad strokes. In the kitchen, lights were on. This hour of the day was an ambient glow, not powerful enough to illuminate. It simply *was*. And it was Rhett's favorite. Before his brother and father's arrival, it had been a time for sipping scalding chicory and listening to the muffled outside, while scrolling the weather app for the day's predictions. Few thoughts. Maybe a cat joined him.

Tom shook his head. "You gonna complain if I make dinner again?"

"No. But I don't care if you sit with your thumb up your ass all day, either. Besides," Rhett waved towards where Callum still slept, "you've got him."

"Speaking of him. I might not be able to keep him out of the stables today."

Around the handle of the mug, Rhett's grip tightened.

"There's no reason he needs—"

"I know. His knee bothered him yesterday so I could reason with him." Tom shrugged and poured a cup of chicory himself before sniffing it and adding stevia. "But I'd like to save tackling Dad for bigger moments."

"I'd rather get kicked."

"That's not fun, either."

Mid-pour of a second cup, Rhett looked at his brother. "Has he?"

"I told you. When he gets lost, it's like his body is fighting anything it can reach."

Rhett emptied the cup. This shouldn't be part of the bargain. To help someone who doesn't want help. To take the upper hand with a parent and tell them what they need when they never gave...

No. Don't go there.

He strode from the kitchen. "Anything but chili, okay?"

After getting inside the Jeep, dust followed by soiled clouds plumed as his foot hit the accelerator. Driving to the ranch took no more than five minutes; walking might take twenty, though Rhett had run it in ten. The side of him that shook off being bucked by a horse when he was nine accused him of being a little bitch. A real man would have walked there and back each day, seasons confound.

Weeks after renovating the ranch, his office at last looking like an office, he made an executive purchase of the Jeep. By the end of every day his hands would be dry and dusty, callouses ripping open to re-solidify. However, at the start of each day, he could be the man with no dirt under his fingernails, his shirt still buttoned and clean. *That* man drove a Jeep to work. That man was a stable owner.

Blowing air from his lungs, Rhett rolled down the window and eased his grip on the wheel. There was a coffee pot in his office. Most of the horses would still be asleep. He'd get to all the messages Jenny took. The stables didn't open until eight. If the day brought his father, then he'd had peace earlier.

If the day brought Succotash's owner, then he had breathed easy for a few hours.

Parking, he tried not to imagine her.

A lot like the day they first met.

Something in his insides had shifted and it brought the sight of her to his mind's eye so often he started avoiding her if it wasn't obvious. That little thing didn't need to see him, twenty-four years old, ducking around corners. Except being within eyesight of her made him feel alive and dirty at the same time. She looked younger than she was, yet after sifting through her job application, knowing she was nineteen did not ease him.

Nor did it help that she sought him out, asking questions, asking for help, asking him to show her how things were done. No one could possibly muck a stall so slow; she was playing with him. Cassandra was petite but not delicate. And that tore at his nerves. Her body was lithe and resilient. Maybe she poured herself into her clothes, but she kept a horse solid between her legs.

With one hand unlocking the double wide entrance to the stables, Rhett rubbed the back of his neck.

Contented quiet opened towards him. Unseen, lazy, ruffled snorts. Hay crunching and rustling underneath big bodies, blithely asleep to the world. Above, the low whirling hum of the ceiling fans droned slowly. One of the barn cats mewed at his entrance before tucking her head between her paws and forgetting all about him. Damp hay, murky refuse, and that unmistakable smell of wet wrapped around him, broken only by the sound of his boots on the cobbled floor.

For the next hour, he'd get to the messages Jenny left. Scanning which could be replied to as an email, and not a phone call first, Rhett glanced up to ensure he hadn't shut the door.

Even when the stables were busy, he preferred the door open. Callum would have said a good stable owner always has his ears tuned into his horses, listening can tell a lot. As a child, Rhett used to stand in the middle of the pasture and listen, imagining himself a superhero horse understander. Matt teased he kept his office door open because he secretly wanted to do everything himself. While that wasn't an unfair accusation, the answer was less about being John Wayne's right hand man in a Ford film than it was how much Rhett would not trade a chore jacket for anything.

Over the years, people had asked what he would do if running a ranch was no longer an option. The question generally came as a joke. There had been a few women, a very few, who complained he talked of nothing else. Worse, that he was incapable of finding conversation not revolving around manure and new research developments on feed.

Regardless, his answer was always the same: nothing. This life was ingrained into him. He was as much obsessed as his father had ever been. This was the lone similarity to Callum Rhett accepted because he could not deny it.

From around the doorframe, several emails fired off to clients he knew would send three more in reply, he heard the wide, double doors open.

"In here, Matt!"

"You're not reading one of the horses a good morning story?" asked a sultry voice, rich enough to send shivers down his body.

She appeared in the doorway, fresh and looking like early morning light clung to her shoulders and arms, reluctant to let go now she was indoors.

"Good morning, Rhett."

Dressed in jeans and a dark green button down, unbuttoned to reveal a black halter bra, her appearance snagged words in his throat. Epona in the modern world; her refuge was for horses alone.

"Stables don't open 'til eight."

Cassandra folded her arms, and leaned against the doorframe. "Okay. I can play by the rules. I'll wait in the car."

She did not turn to leave. Instead, she watched him, and he strained not to drown in those April blue eyes.

"Suit yourself."

"It doesn't. But I can be good."

Like brush fire and high-water she could be good! What was worse? Knowing she sat outside his vision and no amount of head turning would be enough? Or, that he could see and hear her? Neither and nothing. In her presence, he lost every time.

"Quit. Hang around, if you want."

"You sure?"

"Do I sound like I'm not?"

A soft smile played at her lips. "No, Sir."

"Fucking go wake up your horse. Tash sleeps like a log."

"She's a smart gal," she said, walking away.

So are you. What kind of game is this, Cassandra? I'm not gonna believe anything you say. You come back just to see if you can win me over again? Fine. Done. I'm won.

"Maybe I'll get a white flag and wave it in your face," he mumbled to himself, watching her walk away, and then closing the office door.

A PERSISTENT CASE OF rain rot had Rhett in the stable of the ranch's Chincoteague Pony, Molala. Molala's owner did not frequent the stables. However, when she did come around, she expected her pony's surroundings to be pristine. She all but got down on her hands and knees to find wet spots in the hay, before giving her tiny mare a more thorough once-over than some breeders.

The infection contagious, her scabs oozing, Rhett had been spraying a benzyl peroxide topical against the grain of her fur for three days now. However, it wasn't clearing like he wanted. Speaking softly to the sturdy pony, he apologized for her discomfort. Checking to see if the dense cremello colored fur was saturated, sharp words drew his attention.

Callum yelled.

Apparently, Tom couldn't keep him in the house. Figured. It was a good day. High sun, minimal clouds, and a steady wind to keep them from piling up.

So, the big man came down to the stables that used to be his. The ones he built with his own hands, a hammer, nails, and the sweat on his back. The story got old.

The ranch was supposed to go to Tom. Eldest son, carrying on the Farris name gonna have a mess of kids and a wife who was never not pregnant. There was room to grow Saratoga on this land. Any horse owner in the tri-county area knew the Farris ranch was the best.

Except, even though Tom grew up breathing the same shit as his younger brother, his lungs couldn't take it. July in Wyoming left him slumped over in a saddle. He tried to explain to Callum, said it felt like breathing through a soaked hand towel that had been boiled. However, none of his protestations were believed until he fainted dead off a horse one day.

Aware his grip on the spray bottle tightened, Rhett tried to curb his breathing and listen through his pulse's pounding. It sounded like his father was yelling at someone, the tone familiarly accusatory.

Moving quickly, ready to be angry, worried this might be a violent spell, Rhett left Molala.

Before Callum Farris, imperial in a denim button down, stood Wyatt Brown, high school bareback bronc prodigy, looking all of eight inches tall.

"You stack hay bales like your brain is stacked wrong, boy!" Callum thundered, pointing behind Wyatt to a loaded three-wheeler.

"Yes, Sir."

"You teach yourself to do a mess job like this?"

"N-no, Sir."

"Who taught you to stack them bales like you're slow in the head?"

Rhett stood alongside Wyatt and placed his hand on the teen's shoulder.

"I did, Dad."

Callum folded his arms across his chest, and under his father's appraising gaze, Rhett waited.

"That's not how I taught you," he said, evenly.

"Nope." Rhett moved between his father and Wyatt, turning to face his young employee.

"Mr. Rhett," he started, "I can re-do these."

"Don't. It's fine. Get back to work."

All arms and legs, he scrambled into the driver's seat and peeled backwards out of the barn.

"*Mr. Rhett*," Callum scoffed. "How's that feel? Bein' the big man? The man with the plan?"

Rhett shoved both hands in his pockets. "Feels like work."

"You sure worked to make things look different around here."

There was one night, angry and bitter as piss and vinegar, Rhett sat alone in his room. Seventeen-year-old muscles and emotions straining, he swore he'd never strike his father. No matter what, he'd never be that son. But damn if he didn't want to.

He'd been angry about Tom. His father wanted him strapped in leather and belt buckles when his body was better suited to an office. Callum Farris didn't see that, though. He saw the eldest, first-born and future of the family. Inwardly, it ate at Rhett, knowing his father might never be made to understand.

Like he wouldn't understand now, and it was better to give a half-ass answer than really try to say anything.

"I work. I think that's about it."

Before his father could answer, arms still folded, hackles raised, and ready to prove his masculinity to his son, Rhett walked away, as if no electric charges raced between them. However, he was nearly at the end of the stables before he pulled his hands from his pockets.

THE CLOSEST NEIGHBOR to Saratoga Ranch was a heritage turkey farm. Around the holiday season, Dave Parker would come over with one of his year's finest and Rhett would joke he needed to start weaving wreathes from horse hair to offer something in return. Dave, a wiry man who looked like he'd never eaten a shred of meat in his life, would laugh, clap Rhett on the shoulder, suggest seasoning for the bird, and drive back down the road.

Late afternoon had blown in with the low-slung heat of a lowering sun. The horses had been turned out, and Matt was dealing with a few unexpected clients. Seated behind his desk, Rhett's attention was on spending spreadsheets when his phone rang.

"Saratoga Ranch. How can I help 'ya?"

"Rhett. It's Dave."

"Hey there. What's up?"

"A coyote got one of my hens last night."

"Oh, I'm sorry—"

"Must be a break in your fence."

"I'll ride out and check now. I'm sorry about that, man."

"Heard them screaming, but I couldn't get outside fast enough."

"I'm hanging up and saddling one of my boys right now. I'll get it fixed."

On the way out, he hollered for Matt to hear that he was checking the fences. Striding towards the pasture opening, Rhett put his middle finger and thumb between his lips and under his tongue before blowing a shrill, clean whistle.

Horses know how to come. Like dogs, though, some are less eager to please. However, Ben would go a long way for wither scratching. It took a few minutes, but soon the seal brown body, with black mane and tail, trotted towards him.

"There's my good guy."

The big head, with ears relaxed, dropped down and pushed into Rhett's chest.

"Let's get you tacked up. We got work."

Astride the broad back, Rhett guided his gelding towards the pasture fence line. Likely the break was on the left side where their lands met. Regardless, Rhett would walk the perimeter. Horses play-fight. Big, powerful bodies can cause big damage. This also would not be the first summer idiot drunks, out camping, had cut wire for shits and giggles, hoping to cause a stampede.

Warm wind, scented with grass and earth, moved around him and Ben, ruffling the black mane and his shirt. Heavy hooves from the lumbering body clumped down into the ground, accenting the lilt and tilt of Ben's gait. The air, the sounds, the feel—all of it was like sleeping and waking, carefree thoughtlessness. Circadian. An organic kind of automatic he'd never tire of.

Color from the corner of his eye turned Rhett's head.

Fuck me.

She hadn't tacked up Succotash, and lay, legs astride the mare's neck, on her back with one arm draped over her eyes and her hair left to the wind's devices.

You were laying like that one day, Cassandra, when I pulled you off. You said you fell asleep, but I didn't believe you. I think you knew what you were doing, aiming Tash to walk past me. I slipped my arms under you and pulled you to my chest. I was gonna carry you over my shoulder and tease you about the right way to ride a horse until you grabbed my face and pulled my mouth down to yours. That's when I took both of us down into the grass. Tash was polite enough to stay close but not watch.

You pinned me. I let you. Your hair, grass and twigs sticking out. Sun low on the horizon. Good God, did I love you.

But you wouldn't wait, and you didn't understand. I was twenty-four and you were nineteen. I wanted and loved you like a woman, but I...

She had all but tried to strip him, seduce him, and make him lose his mind. When her plan failed, the accusations she hurled were ugly. If he couldn't get in bed with her, stand the idea of seeing her naked, then he didn't love her. She accused him of keeping a slut on the side. Or that he was fulfilling some sick sexual fantasy where he made her insane for his body and left her to burn. Once she told him she had a one-night stand with another man.

"There. Now you're not first. You don't have to worry about soiling the virgin. Take me."

Then and now, he'd never been sure if that was a lie. She was rank enough to do it.

Over and over, he begged she be patient with him. Yes, her age mattered. If he was so important to her and she wanted him so much, then couldn't she wait 'til she turned twenty? Couldn't they wait? Weren't they worth it to one another?

Guess not.

Days before she turned twenty, she picked an awful fight with him, and the next morning, he learned she was gone.

Lifting his chin and exhaling, as if to blow those jagged memories away, Rhett tapped Ben's sides and the big bay picked up his pace. He needed to be looking at the fence, not backwards in time.

CHAPTER SIX

A big horse for a big man. A handsome bay draft guided by a darn good-looking man. Cassandra watched Rhett ride and wondered what his horse's name was, wondering, too, if he'd seen her. Probably. He kept watch on the horses under his care. So, he'd seen Succotash and chosen not to say anything.

With little difficulty, she sat forward and then scooted higher on her mare's rump, hooking her own legs behind herself and then laying down on her stomach, head turned to keep Rhett in her sights.

Of course, he hadn't said hello. You don't say hello to strangers. Five years was a long time to stay away from a life and the man he'd grown to be no longer recognized the woman who had come back. Because she wasn't the girl who left. That girl was angry and hurt. She refused to believe what he said and didn't accept him for who he was.

Although, back in New York, she thought she understood Past Rhett a lot better. Now, dropping into his life, that understanding did not go far.

Rhett Farris was a principled man. There was a right way to do things. There was a decent way to meet each new day and he did his best to stay in the right.

Still new to the ranch at nineteen, Cassandra gawked at the owner's son, quietly working, his energy even-keel and unwavering. Fatigue might be clear in his expression, but he stayed steady. Constant. She wanted to get closer to his stability.

More to the point, she wanted to be surrounded by his strength.

At first, it was adorable how distracted and uncomfortable he was when she lingered. Over their relationship, she learned what hid beneath his restlessness. His need and attraction were intoxicating. She couldn't get enough.

Yet, in urging him to satiate her, they hit a snag. Here she was, with all this womanly longing, ready to ride him into the dawn, and he said she was too young. She used to tell him she'd prefer he strike her then say he couldn't sleep with a nineteen-year-old. If he loved her, then prove it. If they were gonna spend a lifetime together, then what was stopping them? *Him*! And she resented him for it.

Pushing herself upright, Cassandra patted Succotash on the shoulder and the mare went from idle ambling to a consistent walk. Overhead, the wind brought billowing clouds, sweeping, and swirling their shapes from mountains to dollops of whipped cream. Tash's hooves clomped through the firm dirt, and Cassandra let her seat, her riding posture, go, leaning and tipping with the sway of her horse.

Throughout the craze of moving, she told herself she understood Rhett now. Time had offered her comprehension. Although, it didn't make him right about abstaining. She knew her mind, now and then.

However, her desires were turned so far inward she didn't see a man fighting to do what he thought right. She saw his urges and needs, yet didn't see how much strength and force of will it took for him to abide by what he considered right.

And no matter what she accused him of or how she tried to undermine him, he'd remained firm.

At the time, she saw it as an affront. Not until she was in the middle of arguing with Martin, making arrangements for Tash to be ground shipped, did she realize what his refusals meant. Dedication. Dedication so doggedly strong even words of a loved one could not alter him.

This, this was the man she wanted. One whose foundation was carved from granite.

Back in New York, she imagined their first meeting a dozen different ways, most of them with Rhett's expression stern. However, she told herself being around him and part of stable life once more would soften the hurt she left in him. It had to. Horseflesh was his life, and it was hers. Both of them had scars from ill-tempered animals. On their hands, both had callouses thickened, torn, and thickened again. He belonged to the land and though she'd taken the prodigal route, this red clay dust lined her lungs.

She tucked her heels into her mare's flank and the gait changed.

"I need some of this wind, girl," she said aloud, knowing Succotash preferred to walk or gallop, not limbo at a canter.

Succotash shook her head.

"Just cause we're not working yet doesn't mean you get your way, smart thing. Push me more and we'll go through all the gaits. You feel like lunging today?"

The answer was a snort.

"That's what I thought."

Tash hated lunging. Her high-minded self found being asked to practice different gaits at the end of a line, moving in and out to fine-tune rhythm, humiliating. She was better off-lead and listening to vocal commands. Spectators would never know how much time it took and the special sort of horse her girl was to respond to voice direction.

The creamy white ears turned. Cassandra looked over her shoulder, seeing Rhett, the sight of him reaching her before the sound of his horse's hooves did. From a distance, she watched him dismount and then shrug off a backpack. For a moment, she let the hungry side of herself enjoy the way those shoulders moved, the shirt he wore barely masking the musculature underneath.

Out of the backpack, he pulled a roll of wire mesh, and it was then she noticed a break in the fencing.

With a tongue cluck and a gentle tug on the reins, Cassandra turned Tash to ride towards him.

On his knees, he sheared wire mesh to fit over the gap. Momentary indecision pricked at Cassandra. He'd heard her approach and chosen not to look.

Suit yourself, then, Rhett.

Laying the reins over her mare's withers, she swung down.

"Need a hand?"

From behind, sunlight pooled her shadow over his body, and he looked up. On his hands and knees, his eyes the color of early spring breaking through the earth, he looked at her and she fought the urge to step back. Earnest clarity undarkened by the shadow she cast so poignant, it struck her sternum, threatening her balance.

"I've heard two heads," she started, clearing her throat, "are better than one."

"Pretty sure I can handle this."

Regaining her composure, she squatted down. "You sure?"

"When's the last time I couldn't handle something?"

Aside from me? Never.

"You've always been good with your hands."

For an instant, she thought a smile played on his mouth.

"I thought you came out here to ride, Cassandra."

"I did."

"Well?"

"Well, I saw you, and I wanted to stop riding. Say hello."

"You wanted to play games."

"I'm not playing games, Rhett."

The cut wiring was in both his hands, but he set it down, daring her to look away. Heat pushed up in Cassandra's throat. He reached forward, took the section of hair spilling down over her chest, and swept it behind her shoulder, leaving his arm to rest across.

"Now tell me again," he said, his voice low, the space between them diminished, "tell me again you're not out here playing games with me."

"No games, Rhett."

"Bullshit."

She touched his wrist. "Try me."

A muscle in his jawline flexed. "Why are you here?"

"I had to come back."

"To what?"

"To you."

As if burned, he yanked his arm away and sarcasm lined the following words. "After all this time? After you made a life for yourself out there? One day, you up and decided it was time to move across the country?"

"It wasn't quite that simple, but—"

"Bullshit."

Picking the grating up, he turned away and placed it to fit the tear.

"It's true whether you believe or not."

Zip-ties between the fingers of one hand, he shook his head. "I used to believe a lot of things."

There it was. A dig. A neat little smack that stung more than she expected, despite knowing she deserved him saying much worse. And knowing he might still be too much a well-bred, country-western boy to say it smarted further. Every ugly name in the book she had earned and any number of accusations he'd be justified in hurling at her, except he wouldn't because he was too much of the right kind of man.

Cassandra stood.

"I've got time. I'm not going anywhere."

Glancing over his shoulder before giving the temporary fix a tug, he pulled two more zip ties from his pocket and asked, "That a threat?"

Cassandra patted the side of her leg and Succotash, who had meandered to munch grass, walked towards her.

"You can call it whatever you want."

She swung up and he stood to face her.

"I think I did call it."

"Bullshit. I heard."

"But you don't listen."

Ouch. "Nope."

He came alongside and slapped the honied rump. "Take your mama home, Succotash. Go on, get!"

Tossing her snout in the air, the mare whinnied and pranced her front legs before obeying the voice she, too, knew so well, taking her rider away at a gallop.

INSTEAD OF LEADING Tash back to her stall, Cassandra dismounted at the entrance to the smaller paddock. There she unfastened the saddle and slung it over her shoulder and arm, leaving the bridle in case she wanted to be spicy for anyone but Rhett calling her in.

Late afternoon at Saratoga Ranch. Stalls had been mucked and freshly bedded. Gallons of water tumbled into troughs for when horses came in for the night. Mixtures of feeds and supplements poured into feeders, the sound a never-ending topple of dominoes. Ranch hands bustled, calling and laughing at one another. Heat from the day's sun warmed the wood, the hay, and the feed, tempered only by the fresh breeze scent of clean water.

She loved it. New York and here, but here more so. The Adirondack stables catered to an elite crowd. Over her first days of working there, Martin informed her the clientele wanted to see what their money went towards. She needed to lose the whole "cowgirl" look and stock up on high-waisted black slacks and white button-down tops. Her skills had gotten her in the door, but these stables had a reputation she needed to resemble.

At the time, she threw herself into the eastern saddle expectation. Black velvet riding helmets and regular appointments at the salon for manicures and blowouts. She bought an iron. Clean, polished, and proud, she and her mare. All white gear for Succotash, her mane and tail meticulously braided at shows. Already an unconventional breed for hunting, no one was going to stare down their nose at her girl. If people talked, it was about what a beautiful team they made.

And that was still true but different here. Cassandra's hair was out of buns and French twists, a red blur over her shoulders and down her back. Succotash could feel the wind in her mane again. Both of them preferred a Western saddle. There had been no ceremony throwing away the iron and she sold the white gear for half its worth. To get home to jeans, dust, and space.

And Rhett.

" 'Scuse me, ma'am?"

A slim, blue-eyed girl motioned. Caked mud smudged her shirt, hands, and face. Happiness, however, shone in her expression.

"Can I do something for you?"

"Oh, no! I meant," she reached out both hands, "I was wondering if I could help you carry that tack."

Cassandra smiled. "Sure."

"I'm Jenny," said the girl, taking the proffered reins and stirrups. "I'm working here for the summer."

"Hi, Jenny. I'm Cassandra."

"I know. That cream and honey is yours, isn't she?"

"That's right."

"She's a beauty."

"I think she knows it, too."

At the door of the tack room, Cassandra waited while Jenny put away Tash's things, handling the reins and stirrups almost reverentially.

"She's got gorgeous markings."

"They brush up good."

"I bet."

"See for yourself sometime. Succotash loves a good brushing."

Jenny's smile might make a daisy blush. "I was hoping you'd let me. When Mr. Rhett brought her in, I almost shoveled my own foot off. She's perfect. Like someone painted her."

Cassandra was about to respond when a tall figure loomed over Jenny.

"Am I that old and senile or is that Cassie Verlice?"

Quick, like a field mouse, Jenny ducked and scurried away. Callum Farris had that effect on people.

Hers had been a similar reaction, but how quickly he became a gruff, kindly bear in her eyes. His was not a surly outer shell shielding tender sensibilities. Callum was a brusque man. However, that did not blind Cassandra. A quick arm around her shoulder. A wink on hard days when she felt she could do nothing right. His voice boomed when his frustration and impatience flared but she'd stand under the torrent, and he'd pat her back wordlessly and walk away.

For her he made no exceptions. To her he gave Succotash. When her relationship with Rhett grew obvious, she feared Mr. Farris' disapproval. A man like him, with a budding romance under his nose, within his horseflesh empire? Inwardly, the first time they walked past Callum, his son's arm around her waist, she shrank. Yet, all the big man did was look at her and wink.

Seeing him now, still the towering patriarch lacking a kingdom to rule, he stood with the command she believed inherent, but a haze had clouded him in a way she couldn't explain to herself. He was the same, but was something missing. Or had something changed?

Wide arms he held out to her, and she stepped inside.

"What planet did you blow down from, coming all the way back here?"

"Not sure you've heard of it," she said, grinning. "It's called New York."

"Sounds far away."

"Too far, turns out."

"Roots don't always hold you back. They can help you grow better."

"Lesson I needed to learn on my own."

"I could've told you, though."

"Oh, I know that."

He winked and then asked, "You got somewhere to be, or can you walk an old man back to his house?"

"You're not old, Callum."

"Feels like it, sometimes."

"Bet you can still out ride me."

He laughed. It wasn't a sound Cassandra thought she'd forgotten but it brought her to quiet nights under the Farris roof when Callum complained there was never enough salt on his food or Tom sneezed repeatedly if there was too much hot sauce in the egg, sausage, hash brown casserole.

An ache near her heart made her grab his hand, like she might contain the hurt and prevent it from spreading.

"Lead the way."

"You spent too long in New York and forget?"

"No. I remember."

Everything.

THEY SAT ACROSS FROM one another in the living room. Callum in the same armchair that looked like it had been a bargain basement deal when in was new in the early 80s. Except it had been reupholstered. Dingy brown leather had vanished, replaced by an espresso colored fabric. In fact, all the furniture had been revamped. Under her feet there was still a rug but not the one she remembered. On the walls were all the same paintings, awards, and portraits but the walls had been painted in tones of oat milk. The house she knew was the same but different, the contrast struck a paradoxical chord woven between her ribs.

Rhett was still the man who cared for her. Was he the man who wanted her back, though?

With a mental shake, she refocused on the conversation. Callum had been telling her about the last few years and there were unexpected phrases. Medication routine. Fog and clear. Dissociative cognizance. Early on-set dementia.

Cassandra sat forward, leaning her elbows on her knees.

What? Callum Farris at the beginning of dementia? This lumbering man, age could wield no strength against, victim? His hands were steady, his eyes clear. More salt than pepper colored his hair and beard now, true. More lines wrinkled at the corners of his mouth and eyes, yes. Yet no grandfather slump caved his posture nor had withering weakness robbed his voice of command.

Staring at him, she wanted to deny and rail against it all. However, she heard resignation in the march of his words and saw somber reality reflect in his eyes.

In her own, Cassandra felt hot tears sting.

"I just can't..." she began, blinking furiously.

"Now, don't you get on over me. I ain't a drooling fool, yet."

Forcing a laugh, she intended to say he'd never be a drooling fool, but the front door blew open and shut with a bang, Rhett striding inside. Phone to his ear, mid-conversation, he glanced at Callum before his gaze fell on Cassandra.

"Cassie's back home."

Like he stood under a predator's stare, his only hope for survival in moving slowly, the hand holding the phone lowered. A voice on the other end said "hello" three times before Rhett ended the call.

Crossing one leg over the other and lacing his fingers together in his lap, Callum furthered. "Put that phone down and sit with us."

The answering look Rhett shot his father was violent and Callum's continuing calm expression was somehow more unsettling. Power struggled here. Who was right and who needed to get in line. Who was man of the house? Unwittingly, she'd stepped in the middle.

I love you, Callum but...

Cassandra stood.

"I should get going. Aunt Louise was so generous about me not paying much in the way of rent, I feel like I need to fix her dinner before she gets home."

"She still working at the library, Cassie?"

"Yes," she replied, looking at Rhett whose gaze had now shifted to his father.

"You're a good girl, Cassie. Get movin', then."

She willed Rhett look at her, but the hazel eyes had set to stone.

"Good night, Rhett."

The hand still gripping the phone moved in acknowledgment of her voice.

CHAPTER SEVEN

Her hand touched his bicep, as she moved past him and out the door. Brief but not gentle. Nothing was gentle about that woman. And neither was the reaction his body had to the feel of her hand. Through the shirt, the pressure of her grip wrenched his stomach and closed his rib cage. If her hand had lingered, he would have pushed her away before his insides deteriorated.

"Good to see Cassie again."

Against his father's reclined, relaxed posture and tone, Rhett steeled himself.

"Yup."

"I missed that girl."

"She seemed glad to see you."

"It was good seeing her in the stables, in the house. Like old times."

"I bet."

Callum's expression maintained a maddening clam. "Seeing you two—"

"Alright. That was five years ago. Leave it."

"Like you did?"

"I..." His heart thundered, rattling bones and thrusting blood through his veins with a vengeance. Rhett strained to keep his voice even. "I'm not getting into this with you right now."

"You didn't get into her, either."

His vision blurred. Was that a challenge? A challenge to what?

Sitting across from him, damn calm, like the world operates when he pushes the button. Yeah, his father liked to push buttons. Alright, fine. He wanted to find the right combination and ascend the final steps of masculine martyrdom by his own flesh and bone striking him?

I'd like to see you fall.

Unsure if his words would come without grabbing Callum by the collar and hoisting him off the chair, Rhett lunged forward. Looming, arms crossed over a heaving chest, his words came slow, "Watch your mouth, *Dad*."

"In your house, huh? That what I'm hearing? Big man in the big house." Callum stood. "The big house your daddy built for you."

Thunder rumbled between them in a moment played across stage and film. An aging monarch, still strong, versus his virile son, his own strength inherited and bristling.

"What did you ever do for—"

"Here we go!" Callum threw his hands up. "What did I ever do for you! Gave you a way to live and make money, gave you a start in life other men would kill for. Gave you a lovely gal—"

"The fuck you gave her to me!"

Hard footfall rumbled from another room, nearing fast.

"Clear out!"

Tom stumbled into the room, hair soaked and a towel around his waist. Using his shoulders, he plowed between the two men, leaning into his younger brother with all his might.

"Back off, Rhett!" he commanded. "Go shove your dick in some chicory and back off. I got enough without playing referee between you two."

Again, he shoved him, and Rhett let himself be pushed.

Anger radiated from Tom, but his temper was not what pulled Rhett out of the brewing storm cloud. Fear hid behind the bravado he mimicked. Hurt soured it, too. An adult child responsible for an aging parent, his own life halted in the care.

Previous relationships for Tom had failed. Fault no longer mattered. The precious few had walked. This left his relationship with his father, whose well-being he was now in charge of, and that of his brother. If both those men collided, Tom got caught in the crossfire.

That Callum was wrong, and Rhett's anger justified, mattered little.

Reaching for the back of his neck, Rhett walked from the room.

NEITHER THE NEXT DAY, nor the day after, saw the resurgence of the argument. Just like old times. Kick up dust in the afternoon and work shoulder to shoulder by the morrow's dawn. Not forgotten, nor forgiven, but tossed aside for more important tasks.

However, the next day, the day after, and the following weeks brought a subject not so simply tossed aside. Every day, between eight and noon Cassandra would come, her gait easy as the swing of her hips. Stable hands knew her name. Jenny had big sister eyes for he, and Matt developed the unnerving habit of telling Rhett when she arrived. Like he couldn't feel her.

Heat pushed from beneath his collar if he saw her walking away, thighs and rear raising energies he didn't want any of the horses to sense; they might stampede. Yet if it wasn't the sight of her, it was the sound of the boots she wore, walking across his bones, or catching the scent of her hair.

She never wore perfume, but that mane of hers got washed in headily scented shampoos. Blood orange and shea butter. Honey and bergamot. Rose and clove. If nothing else about her had changed, and he could not find a difference, then the rose and clove was still her favorite.

I liked the honey one.

Her nestled to his side, those aromas drifting from a body already intoxicating, he used to ask why women bothered with perfume if shampoo could smell this good.

You'd laugh. Or you'd bury yourself closer to me and ask if I knew what I was smelling. All I knew is you smelled good.

Everything about you was good.

Mucking a stall with the worst shovel he could find, making the most work for himself, Rhett tried to un-haul how good it was to see her each day. She was in Saratoga again, within arm's reach again.

Not again, though. I don't have the strength for you, Cassandra.

And you don't have to say it. Sure, maybe you are back because New York wasn't right and if I pretend one plus one equals three, I can believe you brought Tash here because there was no other stall for her. Fine.

But when you look at me, Epona, I'd have to gauge my eyes out to be blind enough not to see.

She was better at hiding it than he. Those April blue eyes, big and round as they were, could stare guileless. Usually, he was the one to look away first, but if he challenged her and fought against how she shifted his insides, then she was the one to blink and turn. And in that split instant, he'd see emotion disrupt the naïve expression.

Remember us, Cassandra? Your heart was happy, wild child, and you ran from that happiness.

Most days, though, he fell into eyes the color of a bright winter morning after a night's snowfall and clenched his teeth against the bitter ache in a far corner of his chest.

A real man would confront her. Or, at least, tell her whatever vixen scheme she had in her head wasn't going to work. She could shake that ass elsewhere. But if he sent her packing...

I don't want that, either.

Maybe Tom was right about where he should stick chicory.

CLOUDS HAD BEEN HEAVY all day. Stuck behind his desk, Rhett kept check on the weather app's radar from his phone. He didn't need telling it was going to rain; the air was heavy with moisture and the wind unpredictable; however, he needed to know when. Weather predictions had been pushing this north-eastern cold front backwards for days. With predicted wind gusts up to sixty miles per hour, he wanted everything that could blow away inside. However, he didn't want to lug it all in until necessary, for it would take hands away from other work.

Scanning client accounts, Rhett listened to the hearty, searching reach of the wind tug at the stable.

"You think we should get everyone in early tonight?" Matt asked, retying the bandanna around his forehead.

"I hate doing that. You see the trajectory swing?"

"No, but I don't like the sky right now."

Matt motioned and Rhett followed him outside.

Dense clouds unfurled endlessly, pushed from their obstinate path by the same wind ripping at Rhett's legs.

"What do you think?" Matt asked, yelling over the gusts.

"Yup. Let's get everything inside. Go tell the hands."

Matt rushed back inside, and Rhett lingered only long enough to glance at the small paddock when he heard a shout.

Wind distorts sound. At first, he looked in the wrong direction, yet when the shout licked up again, Rhett turned, and his stomach contracted. Astride Sam, saddleless, his father sat. Arms flailing, covering his eyes and ears, he jostled and yelled. The rope he'd looped around Sam's neck had fallen, if his father even remembered it was there.

Idiot! Mounting a horse, bareback and no reins.

Anger charged panic and Rhett bolted. A demented cloud had suffused his father's brain and between his sudden panic, the weather, and Sam not comfortable with such weight on his back, Callum would fall.

Idiot! Stupid old man!

God! Don't let him fall!

Callum covered his eyes with his arms, crying. Sam's ears were back. His hooves cut into the dirt and his steps hesitated between forwards and backwards. He was a good horse, but even the best has a limit.

Had to be a big man, huh? See if the years are stopping you, yet? Dammit.

A body of honied cream burst into the scene and Cassandra leapt off Succotash.

"Leave him!" Rhett shouted, but the wind sucked his command into its vortex.

With sure hands, she grabbed the looped rope. Not trying to force or box in Sam's motions, she kept the makeshift reins taunt. No doubt, she hoped the grounded feeling would comfort the big chestnut gelding enough to where Callum could be coaxed down.

"Cassandra!"

If she heard, she did not turn around. In horror, Rhett watched her reach for Callum's elbow, but he jerked away with a shriek and Sam's whinny, shrill and wild, turned his blood to sludge. Cassandra lost hold of the reins. Dangerous hooves reared up, clawing the air. Callum's big body floundered forward and back. Over the storm, Rhett heard Cassandra shout his father's name, reaching for him like a mother reaches for a falling child.

Not in time to catch his father, pull Cassandra aside, or grab Sam's reins, Rhett got to them in time to watch his father's fall broken by her body.

Around the chest, she caught him, air expelling from her in a groan. A body more than twice her size flung hers into the ground with the density of a boulder strewn into a pond.

"Get the horse!" she wheezed.

"Shut up!"

His voice breaking over the wind, fragmented panic piercing his reason, Callum cried for help and slapped away his son's hands. Not caring his own hands were harsh, Rhett grabbed his father under the arms and yanked him onto himself.

"Help me!" Callum cried. "He's hurting me!"

"Dad! You're fine. We gotta get inside."

"Where's my daughter?"

"What?"

Wincing, Cassandra got to her knees and pulled one of his father's arms around her shoulders. Carefully, she turned his face toward hers.

"I'm right here, Callum. I'm right here. We've got to get inside."

The strain and discombobulation twisting his face eased as he focused on her. Rhett looked away from emotions rising he did not want to identify and shouldered himself more squarely under his father.

"Up we go."

Callum let himself be aided but then tried to push away from Rhett.

"You don't help me," he said. "She helps me, my daughter, my wife."

Wind lashed through Cassandra's hair, flogged her shirt and pants. Looming thunder cackled. From Rhett to Callum, and back again, she looked.

"Callum, I'm...I'm right here to help you."

"The fuck you are," Rhett said. "Take my keys and get the Jeep."

Again, Callum struggled.

"Rhett, are you sure?"

"Yes! Go!"

Snatching the carabiner from his belt loop, she took off. Rhett watched her for an instant, a blur of denim and red, before getting his free arm more firmly around his father.

"Come on."

Abandonment stole over Callum's features, and he slumped into his son.

"I wanted to ride the horse."

"I know."

"Where did the lady go?"

"To get help."

"Will she come back?"

Muscles in his jaw tightened.

"She'll be back."

BY THE TIME THEY GOT to the house, rain, thunder, and lightening spilled from the sky.

Tom scrambled up from the basement when they barged through the door. His face ashen at seeing them, he rushed forward, saying he thought Callum had fallen asleep after lunch.

"I should have known better."

Together, he and Rhett got Callum back to his room. Down onto the bed, Tom started undressing the big man and told Rhett to get clean clothes. When Rhett tried to help getting dry garments on, Tom shook his head. Real help would come in the form of gabapentin. It was downstairs in the bathroom. One pill, taken with water. Callum Farris needed rest from himself, and Tom needed to call the doctor and ask again about the side effects of this medication.

All the horses were in, Matt said over the phone a short while later. Cassandra had helped. Sam wouldn't be caught, and she took Tash out to lead him in. He'd sent the hands home, telling them to be careful. He planned on staying for the next hour to ensure all the horses were calm.

"Thanks, Matt. Cassandra leave okay in that useless rental of hers?"

"She said she was heading back to the house."

Shit. Why?

He knew why. Back when a relationship surrounded them, he took comfort and pride he never tried to explain to himself in how she cared for his father. His Epona, untethered and wild, her only tenderness for horseflesh, bent willingly to Farris Senior.

And if Rhett had ever cared to be honest, seeing *this* side of his father poured balm on old wounds. Under all the warped wood, horse patties, and brittle leather was a man who knew how to lower his voice. Should children, one day, come to Rhett, he might not have to stand shield in their grandfather's presence.

What a thought.

And it was supposed to have been Cassandra. His wife, his children's mother.

Tom came out of the bedroom. Sweat beaded at his hairline and his breathing was labored. With a grimace, Rhett pulled himself from his thoughts, yet not before glancing out the front windows to see if headlights neared.

CHAPTER EIGHT

R ain spilled over the rental car. Loud enough to invade her thoughts, unceasing to warp any view from beyond the windshield. She still thought of standing outside and letting the storm have its way with her.

Years ago, Rhett rarely talked about his relationship with Callum. Not that he needed to. She had eyes. Sense, too—enough not to say that the man she loved and the one she cared for were not as dissimilar as both wanted to believe. Callum ran roughshod, but Rhett wasn't polished.

Broaching the subject with Rhett only ended poorly. If not in a fight, then he came at her with his masculinity, and she fell victim in his arms, intended words forgotten.

Once, she tried with Callum. It had been an early morning. Usually, he was first to arrive, however, an injury to his foot left that responsibility to Rhett. Yet, that day, Rhett had picked her up and given her the stable keys on the drive over. Apparently, a gelding got loose in the night, and he needed to find it.

At the time, she didn't like coffee, but she brewed a pot in the barn's makeshift kitchen, intending to keep it warm for Rhett. However, barked cuss words alerted her to Callum's entrance, and she remembered spilling coffee on her hand, seeking to pour it so fast and greet her employer, mug in tow.

His thanks were mumbled, quickly launching into how the injury happened. Nodding and listening, Cassandra let him vent, quietly interested in how Callum's and his son's versions of the accident differed.

"What you grinnin' at?"

"Huh? Oh, nothing."

"My foot nothing."

"Just think it's funny. Rhett told me what happened this morning. You and him explain the whole thing differently."

"Rhett don't know."

"He said the same about you, basically."

"Basically?" Callum had chuckled. *"Sometimes, I don't know that boy."*

She'd wanted to reply with seeing the forest through the trees. Maybe get Biblical, (as much as she could) and mention logs and needles. After all, a person can't see what's in front of them in the mirror; they're blocking their own way.

But there hadn't been time. She couldn't think of the right words, and one of the ranch hands came in.

Still, it was as true then as now. Callum had sought her, blind to the pain in his son's eyes. Hazel hardened to stone, Rhett unable to comprehend or forgive what broke in his father long ago.

Sodden clouds darkened. Cassandra looked at the time. It was getting late. Either she was going in the house to see if Callum was okay, or she needed to get back to her Aunt's. Little cars weren't much good under the big storms of Wyoming. However, she didn't understand her hesitation. More specifically, she did not understand why it stopped her.

Indecision had been something to barge through in life. Unsure about her ability to work with horses? Get a job at a stable. Unsure if she could make it in the professional world of show jumping with a palomino when the time-honored traditions of the sport were entrenched so far down a person had to stick their head up their own butt to see the reasoning? Work your horse 'til she's flawless.

Uncertain over whether the man you love still loves you? Get his back to the wall and find out.

Maybe that was it. She'd pushed him. Pushed him in ways unintended and now, seeing herself hesitate, she knew it might be best to give this man room to breathe. She'd come down heavy as this storm, and though she had never seen Rhett break, even the strongest can only heft so much before they crumble.

I was a burden to him then; I'm not trying to be now.

Cassandra jammed the car key into the ignition.

But does he know I'm strong, too?

Throwing the car in reverse, she cranked the wheel and aimed away from the stables. Shoving the gear shift in drive, she ignored the wheels churning up mud, and sped towards the house.

TOM ANSWERED THE DOOR.

"Cass! What are you...you're soaked. Get inside."

With her hands, Cassandra slicked water from her face and clothes, best she could, before catching an instant shiver in the air-conditioned cool of the house. The coffee cup Tom held, he thrust at her before going to a closet and pulling out a thick hoodie.

"Not my fault the driveway to this house is seven hundred feet from the door."

"Your car break down?" he asked, trading the hoodie for the mug.

Pulling it over her head and shoulders, she then wriggled out of her sodden top and bra before pushing her arms through the sleeves.

"No. Although it definitely wasn't meant for this kind of weather. I wanted to know if Callum's okay."

Tom nodded before he spoke. "He's asleep. I'm taking him to the doctor tomorrow. See if he's got anything worse than bruises."

With her foot, she pushed her wet things closer to the door. "Good. My heart about stopped when I saw him."

"Rhett told me you got there before he did."

"How is he? Callum wasn't..." She shrugged, by way of finishing the sentence.

"I think this new medication might need to change or the dosing. Rhett's fine."

For as long as she'd known Rhett, Cassandra had known Tom and she looked at him now, paler than the off-white mug he held.

"What do you want me to say, Cass? That he's shook up? You know damn well he is."

"Where is he?"

He pointed towards the second-floor landing.

Once upon a time, she had the right to come after him. However, she hadn't hydroplaned down the drive for no reason. Plus, she was taking back what she'd tossed aside.

Absentmindedly, she admired the upper-floor remodel. Gutting a few walls and replacing three doors with one had given the area privacy and space.

Space for two, easy.

Along with that thought, though, her foot on the last step of the staircase, an uncomfortable doubt rustled. Maybe that had been the idea. After all, she'd found a new embrace and no woman in her right mind would turn down the strong arms she'd left.

The idea poured sour sensations into her stomach. Another woman? Was she similar or different? Had he fled from redheads and found comfort with a brunette? A woman more docile. A woman less selfish.

And had they, behind this door, spent long hours in the act she had wanted so much from him?

It'd be petty to think not.

Huffing an exhale, Cassandra pushed herself from the railing and knocked. Not expecting to hear a reply, she opened the door and stepped inside.

He stood on the far end of the apartment-like space, arms folded, back to her, staring out the window. The shirt he wore was stretched taut over his broad back. It wasn't the same from earlier. Dark green tee-shirt and loose fitted navy blue sweatpants. For an indulgent moment, she let her gaze drift over him, dwelling on his bare feet before pushing away intruding thoughts of how she'd like to wander in his arms, bare to him entirely.

"Rhett."

Musculature across his back flexed but his position did not change.

Behind herself, Cassandra shut the door and moved toward him. Despite the tenacity of the storm, in his room its punishment sounded far away, like watching a thunderhead roll in over the hills.

So, you keep the weather at bay, too?

"Rhett," she repeated, her voice a little firmer.

"Dad's fine."

"I'm glad." Nearer him she inched, close enough to feel warmth radiate from his body. "When he told me the other day about what was going on with his health, I didn't imagine it could get...like that."

"Yup."

"Rhett."

She placed a hand on his shoulder, and he spun 'round, the force of him daring to push her back. Still, she kept her hand in place. Beyond the window, breaking the dark sky, lightening shattered, peals of thick thunder in its wake. Before her, he stood immobile. Barely breathing. His expression unreadable.

"Talk to me," she whispered, longing to slide her hand down his arm, over his bicep, and wrap it around her waist.

"I don't know what to say to you."

"Let me help you find the words."

Aware he watched her other hand, she placed it on his chest. Yet no sooner had she felt the topography of his pecs, did he shrink away, moving to sit in a wide, wing backed chair.

Following, Cassandra knelt in front of him.

"Don't."

"Don't what?"

"Do this to me, right now, Cassandra."

"It wouldn't be anything if you let me back in. If you'd stop pretending to be dumb. You know why I'm back."

"Do I?"

For an answer, she slid her hands onto his thighs.

"This isn't the time," he replied, the weight of his voice resting on her skin something wonderful. "Today wasn't good for my insides. My heart either."

Reaching further, she slid her hands around his waist and lay her chest on his legs.

"Tell me how."

His muscles tightened and the following exhale was deep. "Not sure I want to describe how hearing my father call you his daughter and his wife made me feel. Or seeing your body protect him."

"Let me back in, Rhett, and we'll figure it out together."

Swiftly, he stood, and she rocked backwards, landing on her butt.

"You haven't changed." His laugh was harsh. "You always pick the worst times to get at me."

"Seems like there's never a right time."

The angle of his jaw hardened, and his mouth pressed into a straight line. Cassandra hoped what twisted and pined for him in the lowermost part of her body did not betray itself in her eyes. But to see him like this, challenged and on the defensive. It was how some of their worst fights ended in delirium.

Outside, bellowing wind thrust rain against the windows.

"What do you want me to say?" he asked.

Cross-legged on the ground, she shrugged. "It doesn't have to be much. You don't owe me anything. I know that. And I didn't come up here trying to seduce you."

He smirked. "You don't have to try."

"I meant, I was worried about you."

For a long moment, he stared at her, eyes moving down her body and back again.

Look all you want. I'll sit here and play eye candy for you. Just let me get close enough to touch, Rhett.

From far in his chest, it seemed, he groaned. Then in nearly one motion, he grabbed under her arms and lifted her to himself, entirely. Around him, her legs and arms crashed, and she buried her face in his shoulder.

To feel him again, so suddenly and fully, she could have wept. Long pent longing slaked its thirst in his embrace.

"Rhett..."

"Shut up and let me hold you."

She wanted his hands down her back, around her thighs and backside. She wanted to hear him say her name like a triumph and an oath. She wanted to trace the lines and cares on his face, replacing each with a kiss. Be allowed to lay her head on his chest and listen to the sound of his breathing and heart beating.

Yet if there was any hope of starting over, if she could prove one shred of true difference to him, then she'd obey his command here and now.

For a long while, he held her. At length, when he set her on her feet, Cassandra grappled not to prolong their proximity When he combed fallen hair back from her face, raking it over her shoulders, she wanted to accuse him of being the flirt.

However, no delightful twinkle lit his eyes. Melancholy still rained down.

He asked if she was going to be alright driving to her aunt's. Quippish replies popped in her mind, but she nodded instead and told him not to worry. He'd done enough of that today. A real smile, faint and faded, passed his lips and he told her to keep the hoodie. It looked better on her than it ever did on Tom or him.

THE SEAT SQUELCHED as she sat down, slamming the car door, despite the wind's fingers trying to yank it backwards.

Welcome home, honey. Storms nowhere else like it does here.

Fumbling with her cell phone, Cassandra tapped out a quick message to Louise, letting her know the rain was going to make the drive a long one and she shouldn't wait up.

Gripping the wheel as if she anticipated the storm would blow her down the road before the car was in gear, Cassandra turned the ignition key. Automatic headlights blinked on, doing little good. Windshield wipers strained across the windshield. She'd driven in worse but with a better car. Before any of this mess with the house was finished, she needed to lease a truck.

With hands at nine and three, she started the winding trek down the Farris driveway. Her headlights barely reached farther than the bumper. Frankly, she'd rather drive in snow than rain. Frozen slick was preferable to silt, mud slippery. In the winter, tires could grip snow. Mud slid.

Her and Rhett had been driving in a storm like this once. Squinting through washes of rain and metronome wipers, she wondered if he remembered it, and if he did, did he remember the fight or the wonderful aftermath?

Earlier in the day, she and Succotash had not placed well in a jumping event. Afterwards, Cassandra had thrown her helmet in the trailer, before loading her mare, and Rhett called her out on it. With a bruised ego, and hurt feelings she was trying to stifle, wondering if she had any talent, his words chafed.

"You didn't listen to the riding master. You damn well didn't listen to me. It's no wonder you placed dead last."

Seething, she'd told him that if he knew how to ride her horse so well, then he should be the one to load Tash and she would walk home and think about her crimes, like a good little girl. Explosive retorts burst from him, but he restrained himself and that surged her temper further.

He turned and walked away. She remembered hollering that a real man wouldn't stand by and hear his woman talk to him that way. He'd do something.

However, his something was keeping silent. So, she stormed off, not caring she still wore her riding habit and the walk back to Aunt Louise's was better than fifteen miles.

And he let her darn near walk all of it. It was night when headlights flooded behind her and a horn honked. Her proud self ignored it. Rhett sped up, jumped the median, and brought the truck to a screaming halt, cutting her off.

He jumped out and blocked her path.

"You done pouting, miss?"

"You gonna act like a man now?"

"You gonna pull up your panties and behave like a woman with some self-respect?"

She'd swung to slap his face, but he caught her wrist and hauled her over his shoulder.

"This what you want? A big brute to keep you in line? I'm not that guy. I got too much respect for you, Cassandra."

On the hood of the truck, he'd plopped her, hands on her waist, keeping her put. He'd demanded to know why hearing the truth had been so hard. If she wanted a punching bag, that could be arranged. However, if she wanted a relationship, then he was here for her.

Convicted by the truth of his words, her response at the time was a whispered apology. Next to her on the hood he climbed, and they watched a Wyoming night sky unfold in dazzling distant sparkle. In and out of embraces, retreating and advancing in intimacy, they spent the night 'til dawn blushed the stars into sanctuary. Sleepy and cuddly, they got into the truck's cabin and drove to a hole-in-the-wall café where the scrambled eggs were as fluffy as the coffee was strong.

I cherished it then but not as much as I should have.

A rain carved dip jolted the car. She felt the wheels turn right and tried to control the spin, feathering the brakes. Still, soaked ground made that impossible and the back of the car felt like it would swing around to the front. With a clunk so hard she felt it under her seat, the vehicle tottered to a stop and the seat belt's safety lock activated.

Leaning forward once like an idiot, she unclipped the restraint, and then grabbed her phone to use its flashlight and find if she could see anything in the swallowing darkness. Even after careful examination, all Cassandra could see was the bumper nicely wedged in a mud bank.

Great.

Walk back to the house like a drowned cat and spend the night on the sofa?

Sit in her own puddle inside the car 'til dawn?

Or call roadside assistance and wait an undetermined amount of time for a tow truck?

Nothing sounded good.

Jilting her boot free from the mess it sank in, Cassandra got back inside. Yet, she'd barely swiped her face free from wet, when in the side view mirror, she saw headlights approaching. Unmistakably round lights of a Jeep.

"Gotta be the hero, huh?"

Steadily, the vehicle lumbered beside hers. When the low beams came on, she got out and Rhett intercepted her.

"You know better than to drive a little car like that around here," he called, voice elevated above the sound of the rain.

"You drive out here to lecture me?"

"Get in."

"What about the car?"

"It stays until morning."

"And where do I stay?"

Under the unrelenting precipitation, the tee-shirt he wore was transparent. His jeans clung to his thighs while water rushed down his arms and off his fingers. Against a strong and sudden urge to catch his face between her hands and kiss him, she clutched at her sleeves and repeated the question.

"You stay with me."

CHAPTER NINE

Back at the house, an emboldened side of himself, with roots in the nature of cavemen, hollered within his primitive brain that he shove her at the bed, damn the past years, and any protestations on her part, because she would wake in the morning, smiling. Rhett grabbed the back of his neck and shoved the taunting thoughts far away, where they belonged.

Still, he had to be honest with himself. Her hair wet, like she may have just stepped out of the shower, a shower they may have shared, and his hoodie clinging to her frame, launched blood flow away from his brain.

With the loss of oxygen, odd wonderment dizzied him. How was this woman, her body a gut punch, here? Not only how was she here, how was she back? And for him!

There are as many men in the world of horseflesh as women. Lots of people live in New York. Cassandra was dangerous on her own two feet and a siren astride a horse. She may have left fools in her wake, but not every man is an idiot.

Who had *he* been? Meek and mild, his balls in a jar in her purse? A guy either so spineless or accommodating he erected no roadblocks. Free as Rhett thought he'd been with her, maybe she wanted a man to stand on the sidelines and watch her win the race. Not question her decisions, not remind her of boundaries. After all, she was so many colors and shapes and patterns, benign might be the only compliment.

Or had the guy beside her been roughshod? Such a force herself, did she realize she wanted equal strength pulling against her? Someone to challenge her. Someone to buck her trend and make her fight for everything she wanted. Men like this didn't listen. Neither did she. Deaf to restrictions and strong enough to break them down when they got in the way, a man like this plowed through the days with her.

Men like this chafed Rhett.

He'd grown up under one.

An ugly thought ghosted him.

A man like the one downstairs, in his heyday. But because she saw *him* with a daughter's eyes, she'd looked towards the next best thing.

Did you think I'd be right enough, Cassandra? And when you found out I'd die before being the man my father is, you left?

No. He'd claw his skin off if he thought about it much longer. She was back and those blue eyes shone for him like the sun on a clear December morning.

So, what's holding me up? Maybe I say "fuck it" to all this prancing around the perimeter and drive the cattle home.

"What are you grinning at?"

"Huh?"

Between deft fingers, she worked her hair into a braid, her weight on one leg and hip swung out to the side, a sodden vision.

"What are you grinning at?"

"Nothing. I'm an ass."

She nodded. "Sometimes, yeah. You're gonna be one here, in a sec, if you don't give me something dry to wear."

The prod was needed. He went to the dresser and pulled a striped pajama set. To the tickled expression crinkling her face, Rhett shoved the top and bottoms at her.

"Aunt Sue is a well-meaning lady."

"So is the butter she puts in her coffee," she teased, smooth as a river rock.

He feigned wit's end. "Sleep naked then."

She opened her mouth, then shut it and Rhett faltered to regain ground.

"I didn't..."

"I know."

"That's not what I wanted tonight, Cassandra."

"I know," she answered, gently, unaware of how the words leveled him.

Not tonight. Not ever before.

Mumbling something about being hungry, he shoved his hands in his pockets and left.

SCRAMBLED EGGS ARE good any time of day. Three brown shelled eggs, from a cardboard container, he cracked into a bowl and used a fork to whisk them together before adding a splash of milk.

As teenagers, Tom used to refuse Rhett's scrambled eggs because his younger brother neither salted nor peppered them. Apparently, Rhett preferred even bland food to be bland. That wasn't it, though. Younger, lack of seasoning was driven by an impatience to consume. Older, he enjoyed the simple taste. And now that summer brought heirloom tomatoes, the late-night snack needed no other accompaniment.

Draining the bowl into a small, heated skillet, he wondered if she might want something to eat. Except Cassandra did not like scrambled eggs. Soft-boiled, or nothing. There were more eggs in the container. Boiling water didn't take long. Yet, watching the pale, yellow pool pop and bubble around the edges, a wooden spoon ready to push the cooking portions inward and swirl the yolk, he decided against it.

A joyless smirk tugged at his lips. So, she could sleep in his bed, but making the woman something to eat was too intimate. He knew the slopes and rounds of her body altered the shape of his pajamas and blankets, but timing an egg was too much to handle.

Because...

Because why?

If he cooked for her, like he'd done in the past, other things, more important, were getting skipped. Who he was after she'd left was both a nightmare he smothered and a memory that gave him rights to buck. Her and that sweet ass coming back, him losing all the blood from his brain. He needed something powerful to force his attention.

Rhett jiggled the sauté pan. With a swift thrust and yank, he flipped the protein pancake. Grabbing a small towel from the oven door, he took it and the pan to the kitchen table. Towel under pan, he grabbed a fork and cut the round into quadrants.

From Cassandra, he needed answers. Deserved them. The bomb had exploded in his lap, and she was miles away from the blast zone. Although the sight of her was balm, he needed more.

Blowing perfunctorily on the wedge of egg draped over his fork, Rhett owned he did not know what answer he wanted. She wasn't the type for declarations of love, and neither was he.

She came back, jackass. Ditched a life she'd built from nothing. You want that woman on bended knee, or something?

Done eating, Rhett put the dishes in the dishwasher then quickly filled and quaffed a glass of water. A woman in his bed didn't mean the sun wasn't coming up tomorrow. He needed sleep.

Thoughts too fast to catch zipped through his mind.

He should sleep in the living room.

He should grab clean clothes and bed downstairs with Tom.

He was going to throw open the bedroom door, take off his clothes, and shower before climbing onto his mattress.

Back inside the bedroom, sight of Cassandra swept his mind clear. Red braid strewn across dusty blue pillows, her head turned the opposite way, with her lips barley parted. Her arms were askew and the blanket up to her hips.

She slept hot. Always had and teased him she would want the windows open in January when they were married.

Rhett flipped a switch on the wall and an overhead ceiling fan churned. As it gained speed, he pulled a top and bottom from his dresser before going into the bathroom to take a long, tepid shower.

Eventual sleep found him. From a sofa, one leg draped over the arm and one arm draped over his eyes, he waited for it in the still darkness. The storm was moving out. Lightening no longer sparked the interior and thunder grumbled miles away. Part of him longed for the storm to anchor his energy and drown his emotions.

Shame the ceiling fan was so damn quiet.

STIFF-NECKED BY MORNING, his first glance was out the window. If a man lives and relies on the land, then he needs to know what can affect his livelihood. Condensation beaded on the glass. It was already a hot day, then. When he and Matt brought in the horses from turn-out, they would hose them off. Spray more fly repellent, too. Mindy Horse would need her face shield today, protecting her white fur from UV rays.

However, as all those need-to-dos flitted through his thoughts, he turned to look at the bed. Cassandra still slept, in much the same position, though the blanket had been kicked off and her legs were twisted in the pajama bottoms, revealing her calves.

Song of Songs in his bedroom. He'd avoided that book in the Bible until he was seventeen. Too much to think about.

Feeling like an adolescent hick, titillated over the sight of a woman's body not covered by clothing, he hurried to dress. She could wake when she wanted. He would brew coffee for her and leave the pot on, yet not before he had consumed a mug or two of chicory. Something needed to scald his insides and bring the blood back to other extremities.

"You look like shit."

"Good morning to you, too, Tom."

"Want oatmeal?"

"Not if you're making it with rolled oats."

"Steel cut. "

"Don't put brown sugar in, then."

"Food blander than dirt coming up."

Rhett reached for his chicory and began spooning dollops into a fresh coffee filter.

"How's Dad?"

From a canister, Tom poured oats into the bubbling water, quickly stirring them 'round with an over-sized tablespoon. Against the pot's thick glass, its metal clinked like a dull silver bell.

"I'm calling the doctor as soon as the office opens. We gotta do something about these meds."

"He just got on these, right? It's too soon to take him off."

"It is. But maybe we add something or mess with the dosage. I don't like how it's effecting him."

Rhett scoffed. "You mean there's a better version of Dad?"

Tom flinched, and Rhett instantly wished he could ram his own foot up his own ass. Apparently, that's where his head was.

In his own melodrama, he'd forgotten what his brother had been through in the last twelve hours. Keeper of a parent, his own life and wants suspended, it was a weight Rhett could not heft. While Tom carried this burden, this *shiralee*, Rhett came barging in, ready to hack and hew. Angry only at his father, his words deflected off the old man and struck his brother.

Even for a real man, there's only so much he can take in silence.

"Sorry, Tom."

"Everybody loses their shit."

"Except you."

Annoyance twisted the solemn features "Don't speak for me."

Rhett let it drop.

Later, tucked into a second bowl of oatmeal, light, quick footfall touched Rhett's ear, and Cassandra sashayed into the kitchen. Fresh-faced, hair combed and resting over one shoulder, yesterday's clothes looked new and clean on her body. In the yellow and peach suffused morning haze of a humid day, her round, blue eyes were refreshment and clarity.

Surprise quickly subsided in his brother's face, and he greeted her as if there was nothing out of place about her being in the kitchen. And in another time, nothing about that was unusual. Rhett wanted little more than the same sight every morning, although, in his version, they had come down the stairs together.

Cassandra asked Tom if any "real" coffee had been brewed. Winking at her, he pointed to a second thermal carafe and said she could have all she wanted. He reached to grab a cup for her, but she told him to keep eating.

She knew where the cups were.

Tom invited her to oatmeal, but she declined. Without raisins, specifically golden raisins, oatmeal was well-intentioned wallpaper paste.

"When you're finished with your gruel, Mr. Rhett," she began, not looking at him while pouring, "think you can help a gal get her car unstuck?"

"Better specify, Missy," Tom teased. "Tell him to use the Jeep or he'll try with his hands. He ain't got sense."

Her smile was devious and played first to Tom before she looked at Rhett from over the cup's rim. "I bet he could bare hand it, but it's too early in the morning for me to get my petticoat in a bunch."

"That's why I stopped wearing mine," Tom replied, smoothly.

Sitting at the table with one leg tucked under her ass, she sipped at the morning beverage and made idle small talk with Tom until Rhett couldn't stand how casual they were both being. Shoveling a final bite in his mouth, he told Cassandra he would meet her outside.

It was bare minutes later she walked towards him, waiting in the Jeep. Peals of fog hovered over the ground, and she stepped off the front porch into the misted mire. Before her stride it dissipated, closing back in and around her legs in her wake.

Cloudless climes and shit, walking in beauty. Epona, through a bog, marching onward to save a horse frightened by the unknown.

When she grabbed the door handle, he started the engine.

"Sleep okay?"

"Yeah. You?"

I'd have slept a lot better with you not in the room. Or maybe not. I'd like to say I'd have slept better next to you, but I'm not sure that's true, either. You fuck me up-sides and down.

"I've slept worse," he answered and shifted the vehicle into drive.

Cassandra did not pull the seat belt across her chest.

"The safety alarm will sound."

"You're going too slow for it to go off."

He wanted to snatch away the smooth tone of her comment and shove the gas pedal down. Instead, he reached past her chest and pulled the strap across her torso.

"Old-fashioned."

"Proud of it."

Cassandra must have chosen to play sweet because he knew those were fighting words and she let the statement glide by. Five years ago, the same had been hurled at him as an insult.

He wouldn't take her to bed. He insisted she be twenty. He might as well wait 'til their wedding night, she had scoffed. And when he said that's the way he'd prefer it, those soft, blue eyes had turned to ice. Old-fashioned was the first and least offensive insult. Prudish and perhaps not man enough, or not able to get *it* up came next, followed by her unbuttoning her shirt where they stood, demanding to know if her form had any effect on him.

Plodding along the drive, her car in sight, Rhett didn't believe time had changed her mind in relation to the bedroom. Sex mattered. However, the tart filly he'd known refused to yield over anything, and if the woman beside him now had not learned to listen...

He didn't need more of that in his life.

Beside her car, he pulled the Jeep and told her to try reversing and then going forward. He'd get behind and push.

"If that doesn't work, then I'll tie you up and pull you out."

"Are we still talking about cars?" she teased.

"Little early in the morning to talk about anything else."

"What about later?"

She had one hand on the car door, leaning against it, guileless.

"I've got papers to sign at the house around eleven. I know the ranch needs you, but late afternoons are still pretty quiet, right? Let's go for a ride. That boy of yours looks like he could use exercise."

She pushed off the car and closed the space between them.

"And are we gonna talk about how much Ben loves his alfalfa?"

"No."

She reached for the ends of his fingers, intertwining them with her own.

"We gonna talk about why you're back here, making me lose my shit?"

"You know why I'm back, Rhett."

"No, ma'am." He pulled a lock of hair free from her braid. "I'd like to hear you say it."

"Go riding with me, then."

AMONG THE CLIENTELE at Saratoga Ranch when Rhett first met Cassandra were a few young women with rich daddies. They would come on their three-day weekends with suede jodhpurs tucked into polished custom boots, hair perfectly wound, and smelling faintly of perfume. The crop in their hand was the only thing that would touch the horse.

Callum often sent Tom to be the one to greet them. His personality wouldn't scuff their sentiments. Usually trying to keep his sweaty, dusty ass unseen, Rhett watched these women mount up like a person might get inside a car. No regard. It wasn't a creature with a personality and quirks beneath the saddle they sat on. It was an expensive notch in their status quo.

Yet the first time Cassandra mounted up, the wonder and awe in her eyes was like a child granted her wish of a Pegasus. The impossible dream had come true. He might have loved her then, stalwart and dazzled, a princess with dirt on her hands.

And he loved her still, though he'd tried to carve her from his heart.

A stiff-wired brush in one hand, Rhett raked the grooming tool over Ben's back towards his croup. Brushing a horse before riding was a good habit more riders should take into consideration. Fur tangles like hair. Saddle straps and bridles can yank, making for an irritated horse.

Ben leaned into the brush, and therefore Rhett, pursing his lips and lifting his head.

Staggering back then pushing into the big body before Ben unintentionally pinned him, Rhett laughed and asked, "That the spot?"

The routine also soothed Rhett. If there was time before she arrived, and if it hadn't already been done earlier, he'd happily bed each stall. Routine eased his mind. Some might say that such a long-standing routine could leave the mind open to wandering and if that were true Rhett was glad he wasn't among those with such a problem.

Brushing Ben siphoned the pounding thumping from the base of his neck into the front of his skull. Until he sat with her, Wyoming winds the only thing around them, he did not want to think of what this ride might mean or bring.

CHAPTER TEN

Him astride that bay draft horse...

Did they really need to talk this out? It might be easier to pick up where they left off. She didn't need a ring, and there had to be a courthouse not too far down the road. She wasn't nineteen anymore.

Jeans taut over his legs and the wind playing with what little excess there was in the shirt he wore, cuffs pushed up to the elbows, Cassandra had to check herself. This was supposed to be serious. All the hurt and anger between them needed clearing. Steam heat would only cloud her vision.

Between the drive to her aunt's, meeting the executor at the house, and then back again to change, she tried getting into words what had been coarse emotion. Her sorrow, resolve, and dedication had to come from more than the way she looked at him. "Sorry" wasn't enough. Even though her anger had been partially justified, how she acted was not.

And what was worse, she hadn't cared.

Seated next to the window on the plane back then, by the time clouds obscured her view, Rhett Farris had dissipated, Wyoming was dust, and she had a new life before her. At first, her happiness was forced but it scared Cassandra, even now, to think how quickly she had become happy.

A cold bitch.

So, now, if she bared her heart to him and he said no, then she had to take him at his word, the same as he had taken her actions. The man she loved, then and now, wouldn't give chase. It had cut deep, and it would again, but for once, she owed him her respect.

Taking her foot out of the stirrup and hooking her leg around the saddle's pommel, she spoke over the off-beat 4/4 cadence of their horses' hooves.

"So, where'd you get that big boy?"

"Slaughter line. One of the gals at Blacks and Bays Rescue called Matt. They had funding enough to rescue eight, but Ben was breaking her heart. He had an infected eye growth. The family thought it was cancerous and dumped him." Rhett patted the ample neck. "I would have taken him and eight more if I could have. As it was, I grabbed Sam that day, too."

"Softie."

He grinned. "You'd go broke."

"Oh, no doubt."

Succotash snorted and bobbed her head. Casual conversation during walks weren't her thing, especially beside another horse. She'd have made a terrible trail horse or the unreliable one of a pulling team.

"She's just like her lady," he said, looking forward. "Always ready to go."

"Well, she'll have to cool it because Ben doesn't seem the galloping type."

"So long as we're still talking about horses, give her the rein she wants."

"And when she outdistances you in three full strides?"

"I'll catch up."

"Then we won't talk about horses."

With his free hand, he motioned ahead of them. "Get, then."

Tash barely needed a tap from Cassandra's heels. The instant she felt slack, her hooves clove into the ground. Without effort, she outdistanced big Ben and it was hard not to smile seeing her joy in running.

Glancing back over her shoulder, Cassandra saw Rhett bent low over Ben, grinning. Thunder surrounded them both. Clods of dirt flew up in their wake. Cloven wind took for its price any volume their words might have had, and together they tore the wind apart, leaving it tumble in their wake.

People who write stories liken riding at a gallop to flying, but they've never felt the rhythm shake their bones and pound into their heart. They've never heard the snorting huff of the animal they're astride, knowing full-well the reins between their hands could mean nothing if the animal decided against them. A horse at a gallop lets the human they trust experience what besting the wind feels like, and it isn't flying. It's exhilarating.

Yards ahead, Cassandra brought Succotash down, dismounting and giving her girl the chance to walk off residual energy. Watching Rhett near, she tried not to linger on the sight of him, solid and strong. She needed words, not actions. If she couldn't keep her gaze from raking over his body, the things she truly wanted to tell him would evaporate.

Underfoot, the ground resonated with the heft of Ben's hooves. Breathing heavy enough to spark her fantasies, Rhett reined him in and swung down, a solid wall of muscle.

All her words solidified, and, like a penned mustang filly, he had no sooner turned towards her then she bolted. Throwing her arms around him, as if she fled from their years apart and feared losing him in the lonely interlude. Cassandra buried her face in his neck.

Her name was a grunt on his lips. He caught her around the waist, and they tumbled down to the ground. The feel of him beneath her, sculpted and warm, she found his mouth before he could say a thing and kissed him. She felt him tense. For a terrifying moment, he let go and with her eyes shut tight, her heart begged he not slip away.

Yes, there's so much I want to tell you, Rhett. But give me a break. I've been back for weeks, and the sight of you hurts in the best and worst way. I can't take watching you work. If I hear your voice one more time and don't know that I'm gonna have that voice beside me every night, I'll scream 'til I'm blue in the face! Please, stay with me.

A groan she felt reverberate from his chest into hers brought his arms around her again. His hands over her back, into her hair, and down to her butt, his was not practiced need. His movements were brusque and sudden, and she adored it.

Wheezing from the lock of his embrace, she barely heard him speak, the sound of his voice so close to the way her blood rushed. "If this was a test to see if you can still break me—"

"Not a test." She ran her fingers through his hair. "I couldn't stand it anymore."

"I can't take much more of *this*."

"Then *take* me."

"Cassandra, I can't just..." He found her mouth again, momentarily overcome. "You left," he gasped, turning his head away from her. "I don't know if you get it. What you did—"

She caught his face between her hands. "Tell me, then. Punish me. Yell at me. I'll hurt for you. Make me understand," she whispered, tracing her lips along the line of his jaw.

Her body rose and fell with the heave of his chest. With lips parted, he stared at her, those wonderful hazel eyes smoldering into umber.

"Say something, Rhett!"

A sudden and intense vibration struck Cassandra in the leg. Abrupt clarity vanished the heat burning his gaze. One hand left her body and reached into his pocket. Worry spread over his features.

"I have this set special," he mumbled. "Special notification."

As he sat up, she moved next to him. Still, her body was on fire and her thoughts scattered and blown, but fear etched the lines in his face, and slammed her back down to reality.

He swiped the screen and his jawline tightened.

What had been blazing between them a moment ago was gone and Cassandra struggled against irritation. If she was back to take him, then she needed to take all of him and the situation with Callum was part and parcel. Whether or not his needs should usurp her was not debatable. She would not make Rhett choose between her and his father. Yet it stung to know they could be one kiss away from a bliss so intrinsic between man and woman and a cell phone's notification could wrangle them apart.

Never before had she considered that Rhett's heart might be divided. Duty and desire. Should and could. Cassandra and

Callum. And wasn't his sense of obligation a trait in him she loved? What kind of traitor would she be to cite the same quality as a hurdle between them?

No.

Her ego wouldn't get her in trouble again. It could sit and fester alongside her libido. There would be plenty time for both in the long run.

Rhett stood. "I gotta get back."

"Sure. Of course." She scrambled after. "Take Tash. I'll ride Ben back."

Not looking at her, he nodded and strode towards the mare.

"What happened?" she asked, handing him the reins.

"Tom can't get him under control. He's getting physical."

"Rhett..."

Hoping he would look at her, she caught him by the hand, wanting to offer comfort, though she didn't know what to say.

If she couldn't find the words, then what did it say about her? Pain and nerves stoned the expression of the man she loved and nowhere in her small heart could she find solace to speak. *What a woman.*

With eyes on the horizon, he leaned down and kissed her hand. "I'm sorry."

Her mouth was open to reply, but he drove a smart kick to Succotash's sides, and she bolted.

FROM BEYOND THE DOOR, voices bellowed. All three distinct and painful to hear. For a moment, Cassandra thought better of going inside. Tom had needed Rhett and the both of them needed one another against Callum. For a moment, her hand hovered over the door handle. She'd be in the way. Tom had been taking care of Callum and knew best how to handle him. Communication between Tom and Rhett was practically symbiotic. They could handle this.

However, she'd seen the reflection of Rhett's heart constricting in his eyes upon reading the text and it had mirrored pain into her heart, too. Beyond the door, she was not needed, yet she was.

I'm here, Rhett. I'm here for you and everything being with you means.

With a shove, she pushed open the front door and walked inside.

Titans wrestled.

Sweat soaked Tom's hair. Every muscle in Rhett's body was so constricted he might tear from the pressure. Between them, vile words spewing and arms thrashing, stood a nightmarish replica of Callum Farris. Balance askew, he staggered from leg to leg, bellowing not to be touched or he'd kill them both. The rims of his eyes were red and his skin starkly pallid in contrast. Perspiration poured from his underarms and though he stood like a Cyclops, ready to grapple, his hands trembled.

Neither of the brothers saw her and though she stood diagonally from their father, his focus remained drilled forward.

Tom was talking. "You're gonna fall again. I'll stay over here but sit down."

"I'll do whatever the fuck I want! If I wanna jump from the window so I don't have to look at your fucking face anymore, I will!"

Even if Callum was under a medical haze, the words hurt Cassandra to hear, but Tom only glanced at Rhett and kept talking. "You can do that later. But if you fall now and break your coccyx bone, you're not gonna be able to walk to the window."

Callum's reply was thunderous, and he wobbled towards his eldest son while Rhett stepped slowly to the side.

"You can disown me, too but I'm telling you, Dad, if you don't sit down, you might not have unbroken hands."

Rhett inched behind his father.

"I'll write with my dick! You think..." he wavered. "You like this life, huh? Nurse-maiding me."

Now standing behind Callum, Rhett closed the space between them, looking constantly at Tom. Clearly, he was going to overpower his father and waited for the signal.

Cassandra didn't know if she could watch. Vigor and youth would conquer. Yet, it would be like watching an old grizzly bear, claws overgrown and paling with age, fight for what it sees as its own life, go down like so much muscle and bone.

Tears stung her eyes.

Vile accusations still spewed from Callum's mouth, but Tom kept talking. In the goading, he moved towards his father then looked heavily at Rhett. Yet, right as Cassandra saw Rhett's chest heave an exhale, Callum swung around. Anger and an unnatural haze clouded his eyes. It was not his son he saw, but an adversary whose face was stone, though the rise and fall of Rhett's chest betrayed the true emotion clamoring within his rib cage.

"Come on, Dad. Sit down."

"You ain't telling me what to do!" he yelled, his arm swinging back.

Cassandra ran. "Rhett!"

He saw her, instantaneous and terrified understanding streaking across his face.

"Cassandra, get back!"

His command threatened to shut her down. The thunder in his voice resonated within the core of her bones and it took all her willpower to cast off her body's intention to obey the man she loved.

In-between a wild punch and Rhett, she dashed to shield him, and Callum's fist struck between her shoulder blades. She gasped as air pummeled from her lungs.

"God!"

He caught her and spun around, his back to his father and her in his arms.

"The fuck were you thinking?!"

"I couldn't...let him..." She wheezed. "I couldn't let him hit you."

Locked in his arms, her body pressed to his in safety, his response pulsed within her.

"Reckless woman. I love you."

She felt his kiss, first on her forehead and then so achingly tender on her lips that she could have cried if her lungs bore the strength.

Tom yelled. "She okay?"

Rhett did not answer but lifted her and placed her on the sofa with the command to stay the fuck put. Again, Tom asked if she were alright, but Rhett did not hear him. Towards Callum, staring blank, and suddenly quiet, he strode.

Inwardly, she begged he not hurt him, not take thirty years of anger and betrayed love out on a man no longer in control of his facilities.

Although Rhett's movements were not gentle and barley under control, he still had restraint. At the forearms, he grabbed his father, pulling them behind his back. In an effort, perhaps, to distract, Tom put his arm around their father's shoulder and spoke quietly.

"Let's go rest, Dad."

Silence and a vapid downward stare were the response.

"Rhett, we're taking him down to my room. Bring all his meds and that blanket he likes. Make something easy for him to eat, later. I'm staying with him the rest of the night."

"Got it."

CHAPTER ELEVEN

Tension and hostilities in Cassandra's life had been, long before she could recall, shoved in the background. Her father wasn't speaking to her mother, who wasn't speaking to her sister, who didn't want to hear from anyone. It was easy to make someone mad because the boundary lines of what could or could not be said were blurred beyond belief.

For herself, Cassandra had no issue telling her father she was angry or even telling the woman who essentially raised her that she was frustrated. Her father could shove it and her aunt, in the ageless lament of teenager years, didn't understand.

Upon stepping inside the Farris family circle, everybody yelling at everybody felt like reprieve. Finally! People were having emotions and displaying them shamelessly. Tom griped at Rhett for being such a caveman and Rhett constantly reminded Tom where his foot could nicely fit. Other ranch hands hollered and laughed along with the brothers, alternately taking different sides. In the middle of it all was Callum Farris, the biggest ticking time bomb in three counties.

There were days she couldn't help grinning, listening to tempers ricochet off the walls. Sometimes Tom would ask if she got kicked in the head by one of the donkeys because no one should be smiling shoveling manure. With the freedom of the surroundings, she'd suggest Tom suck an egg, wishing she could explain what made the ranch so special.

Seated on the couch, trying to breathe through the smarting sensation between her shoulder blades, those memories hit differently tonight. Maybe it wasn't all freedom and cavorting. Maybe, like turkeys sensing a male opponent, it had been blustering and strutting because more dangerous emotions stewed.

Rhett could have broken his father's neck. Plain as day, she saw it. Meanwhile, medicated or not, terrible anger brewed in Callum. In the middle of them both, Tom stood, weary. With all the haranguing torn away, her distorted perception of freedom turned out to be wild antagonism.

It came with Rhett, and she'd come back for him. So, along with the man she wanted by her side, she'd take the bitterness wound within him. It couldn't be all thrill and adventure. That, like the early days of Saratoga Ranch, was an illusion.

Before she saw him, she heard him sigh. Fatigue did not slump his shoulders but, instead, wearied the look in his eyes.

Cassandra stood to meet him, but he rushed to her, enfolding her, carefully, to himself.

"I'm sorry."

She cupped his face. "You don't need to be sorry."

"You didn't need to see that."

"Neither did you," she replied, tracing his features.

"I don't have much of a choice, he's my father."

"And I'm yours, so that's that."

Covering her hands with his, he pulled each palm to his mouth, pressing his lips to the center. "Come with me."

Cold shivered down her skin, but warmth flared in the lowermost part of her stomach. Under both sensations, she shivered, allowing herself to be led.

"Rhett," she offered, breathless over a moment she'd imagined a thousand times in joy, anger, and loneliness.

Of all the times to pick... Could you be any more of a man, picking the wrong time for everything? I don't want to be the voice of reason here. I don't want to talk you out of this but, honestly, now might not be the right time. And I don't have a lot in me to talk you out of sex. At best, I think I can question you one time before I'm giving over to every ache.

"Rhett," she started again, intoxicated by the sight of him, "we don't *need* to do this right now. I can—"

"I need you," he answered at the top of the stairs, before sweeping her into his arms like the bride she'd longed to be.

Eyes bleary, heartbeat thundering, she laced her arms around his neck.

"That was your only shot, bucko. Maybe I never told you." She lowered her mouth to his. "But I can't say no to you."

Over the threshold, and onto the bed, they tumbled. Mouths starving and parched for the other. Hard and fast hands, searching for skin, impatient with fabric. She couldn't feel him enough, couldn't kiss him as deeply as she wanted. Under him, she wanted to suffocate. Pinned by his legs, she wanted to feel every muscle of his body come down onto her 'til she was obliterated. Let him thrust her down into suffocating depths. She'd breathe in him.

From her hips and legs, she felt her pants torn away and the moan to escape when she felt her underwear slide down, forced her name from his mouth and in the abstract state of her mind, she wondered if her body would react too soon.

With weak hands she pulled at the collar of his shirt. It brought him to her mouth again, his hands raking her hair and his kisses trailing from her lips down her neck, lingering at her collarbone.

"Take it off!"

"Yes, ma'am."

Through vision misted by desire, she watched him unbutton the plaid obstruction and then grab the tee-shirt by the hem and pull it off.

She'd seen him shirtless before. Hot days. A few trips to the lake. But not like this. Towering over her, chest expanding and constricting as he labored to breathe, he was magnificent. Muscles flexed and prepared to ravage her. He was a Titan stepped off the pages of a high school Greek mythology book.

Except better, for he was flesh and blood, and she a willing captive to his might.

"Humor me," he asked, with a devious smile.

"I am prepared to do just about anything if you don't get between—"

"I want to watch you take your shirt off."

The deep longing in his voice rendered her dazzled for an instant before she sat forward.

"Those pants come off first."

Doing as told, he moved quickly, eyes darkening to an umber made from the earth's core, as he watched her remove the shirt and then unclasp her bra.

"Take me, Rhett."

Primal need flashed across his expression, and he stepped towards her, both hands grabbing her waist. Yet, she'd no sooner moaned from the feel of his grasp then she felt the power drain from his hands. He stared at her suddenly wide-eyed, as if a mask had been torn away, revealing the truth of what was happening.

He stepped back.

"Rhett?"

"I..."

"Rhett, what's wrong?"

Shivers rippled over his frame and though he folded his arms across his chest, she heard his teeth chatter.

"Please, Rhett. Talk to me. What's wrong?"

"Look...look at me."

"I am looking at you. Tell me how to help."

"No! *Look* at me, Cassandra!"

He'd turned his head. Swift yet disbelieving comprehension struck her, and Cassandra looked downwards on the man crumbling inwardly before her.

"What...what happened?"

"What do you mean what happened?" he snapped. "You can see it."

Palms up in deference, she stepped towards him, but he moved backwards again.

"It's okay."

"The fuck it's okay! Is this the man you wanted? Useless in front of the most beautiful woman?"

"Rhett, please."

"Get out."

"Rhett!"

"Get out," he roared, throwing her clothes at her.

THE DOOR SLAMMED, AND he listened to her footsteps down the stairs until a second door shut and all was still.

Rhett sunk to his knees, chin collapsing to his chest. Unable to bear the sight of his naked body, he snatched the blanket from the bed and wrapped it around himself before rolling to his back and pushing his hands through his hair.

God.

God!

He shut his eyes.

All of him had burned to be held between her legs. The sound of her breathing, the sight of her red hair splayed over the mattress, stark in color against her creamy skin, while she writhed for him—he didn't know his own name. There was only this woman before him whom he'd waited to have completely for so long.

In their early time together, he told himself he wouldn't objectify Cassandra by lingering on the thought of her body in his bed. When the moment came, she'd be giving him permission to enjoy her physically. Otherwise, he pleasured in her without her knowledge.

It didn't usually work. He had fantasied about their first time a million different ways. From her being a blushing bride, which always made him grin because that was as far-fetched as horse owners agreeing on the best way to keep a stallion, to her pushing him onto the bed while the wedding guests were still downstairs.

Weeks ago, in front of his eyes she'd appeared, flesh and blood, like a waking dream, and though he tried to keep his body from responding, it was useless. Her figure haunted his thoughts. Sight of her made his palms itch and it was maddening and heady all at the same time.

Indication of him being anything other than a red-blooded male was nowhere. He'd disrobed her practically salivating, obeyed her command to undress with relish, and watched her strip teetering on lasciviousness. Yet, the instant her skin was in his hands, all of her trembling for all of him, an ice pick dropped from the cavity of his lungs and plunged into the pit of his stomach. Its melting water seeped downwards, shocking everything it touched and within seconds, he was rendered impotent.

And afraid.

Afraid!

Of what?

Rhett slammed his fist into the floor.

The fuck was there to be afraid of? Sex went back to origins. This was flesh and blood type shit. Programmed into the body, that want for the opposite sex. This was not a question of want. Even now, flat on his back, unwilling to see his own body, he wanted her.

He'd wanted other women less and still was able to...

Rhett sat forward. Sweat started from his brow, and he covered his face with his hands.

It had been six months after Cassandra left. Matt dragged him to a bar, just to get him off the ranch and out of the house. Rhett didn't drink, but that night, watching couples around the bar, wondering what *she* might be doing and with whom, he ordered three shots of whiskey. Since she'd left, he'd lost fifteen pounds. Food tasted like ash. If he'd eaten anything that day, it was twelve hours before hard liquor hit his stomach.

While that wasn't enough to snap his sobriety, it was enough to loosen the grip he had on himself.

There had been a brunette on the far end of the bar, and he didn't need to talk much. She, happily, carried the conversation. Nor did he need to do much before she hinted at how spacious the back seat of her Oldsmobile was. Things went fast and she was drunker than he. She didn't seem to notice how long he was on top of her before he suddenly got off.

They call it "whiskey dick." That's why he couldn't finish.

A year later, then, what was the excuse? He'd been four months into a causal relationship, and she pinned him down on the sofa at the tail end of a make-out session. Like lightening lit a sky, he realized he wasn't getting much out of their companionship. He broke it with her, flatly, while she sat on top of him, naked and wide-eyed.

From then until Cassandra arrived, there had been no one. He told himself his heart went when she left Wyoming, and no one was bringing it back.

But that wasn't it.

Neither was it the whiskey.

He couldn't...couldn't complete the act.

With a cry welling in his throat, Rhett scrambled off the floor, and strode towards the window. At the same time, he screamed with all the lung power he could assume and threw his fist through the glass panes. When one puncture wasn't enough, he brought down his other hand until little of the bay window remained and his knuckles bled.

I CAN'T GET BLOOD ON the door.

This had been the only thought to stop him before racing from the house and getting into the Jeep. Under scalding water, he'd washed his hands and bandaged them with hydrogen peroxide-soaked gauze and medical tape. And though Rhett didn't remember putting on clothes, he found himself dressed before he started the vehicle.

A hesitant voice of reason cautioned driving might not be safe, but Rhett ignored it, much like he'd apparently ignored everything in his life.

All this time wrenching himself away from what his father preached, he dug himself a different hole and his focus had been so totally on Callum Farris, he didn't see the depth to which he'd gotten. It made him want to retch. In the car, he rolled the windows down and cranked the air-conditioning to keep sour bile juices from rising.

Real men don't have trouble laying their woman down and fucking her so thoroughly she falls asleep with a smile. A real man doesn't shake touching the woman he loves. And if he does, then something is fundamentally wrong. Hamlet's off-color relationship with his mother. Oedipus's marriage selection. This was fucking, Freudian shit people with soft voices and doctorates spoke reverently about behind closed doors.

He didn't hate his father because of what happened with his mother. He didn't resent his father's larger than life presence. If anything, Rhett pitied him because he knew what was behind all that bravado. It shone through sometimes. A loneliness he couldn't wrangle with his bare hands. But he didn't resent his father because there were no hugs at bedtime.

Though maybe that was part of the problem. Rhett had given up caring.

What, so I've had it with my dad so I can't get it up? That doesn't make any sense!

Rhett clutched the steering wheel harder. Faint redness appeared from under the tape.

I'm gonna scare her like this. I gotta talk to her, though.

The image of her face when she looked between his legs might haunt him. It wasn't pity or horror. It was...

He swallowed, blinking back tears stinging his vision.

It was insight, as if all the rough rocks tumbled into place. She looked down and then back at him, suddenly knowing.

Knowing what?

He coughed on a sob.

What made so much sense that she should have that dammed look on her face?

Is that how this goes, now? She's the one who leaves before and now she's the one who understands it all? Bullshit! This, none of this, is my fault. She left because she couldn't wait and...

He wrenched the steering wheel to the right. Car horns blasted in defiance. The Jeep jostled as one tire went up onto the curb, out of traffic, and then rocked when Rhett threw the shifter into park. With a sob, he dropped his forehead onto the steering wheel and wept.

It wasn't that she couldn't wait, was it? No.

Wrapped up in noble reasoning, he was too afraid to get started. And worse, he blamed her, accused her of seducing him or being such a horn-dog, she couldn't keep her legs together. She had done *him* an irreparable wrong and he had licked his wounds for years. Then she comes back, believing herself guilty and he was asinine enough to look down on her.

God!

His shoulders shook and he gulped air.

It was me. It's been me all this time. She was right to walk away from a man who refused to take her in his arms and make her feel like a woman. But she came back. My Epona turned around and rode towards me again, willing to get stared down because I'm such a high-minded ass.

By the time he got to Cassandra's aunt's condo, Rhett nearly broke down the door knocking. When it swung back, Louise had mace ready in one hand and a cell phone to her ear.

"Rhett! What on earth—"

"Louise! I'm sorry, I..." He held up his hands. "Where's Cassandra? I have to talk to her!"

"She's not here, Rhett."

CHAPTER TWELVE

"*She's not here.*"

A hollow ringing flooded Rhett's ears and his eyes rolled back. Like so much dead weight, he collapsed to the floor unable to hear Louise scream.

Out of a suffocating fog, paralyzed between an instant and eternity, he came forward, pulled against his will. Two men bent over him, faces unclear and their voices muffled from the reverberating pitch in his ears. Behind them, hands clasped around herself, stood Louise. He wanted to say something, reach out and apologize, but one of the men guided Rhett's hand back towards his body.

They were talking, asking him to follow a finger with his eyes, telling him not to try and sit forward. He'd hit his head. He needed to stay down. Louise was asking if there was anything she should do. The medic asked Rhett if he wanted to go to the hospital.

No. I want to talk to Cassandra. I've gotta get to where she is.

Again, he tried to sit up.

"Whoa, there, Sir. You're lucky Ms. Hutchins was here."

He nodded to the other tech and Rhett felt hands from behind on his shoulders, guiding him firmly to a supine position.

"You have any allergies or chronic conditions?"

"No."

"Not diabetes or asthma?"

"No." *Just impotency.*

"You're dehydrated. We're going to put you on some fluids and then get you over to the hospital"

"No!"

"Mr. Farris," the technician said, "let us do our job. You were out stone cold, and I'm worried you may have a concussion."

"I don't give a shit if I—"

"Mr. Farris. Watch it."

"I've got to find her!"

The medical professional looked at Louise. "Who's he talking about?"

Her response was quiet.

"My niece."

A look of supreme understanding came over the man's face and made Rhett want to slap him into the next room. If his head would quit pulsating.

"I see. Well, I'm sure Ms. Hutchins will get word to her niece as soon as possible."

A needle slid beneath Rhett's skin, and he felt the momentary burn of saline flood his veins.

"Louise," Rhett began, despite the men hoisting him to his feet. "Where did she go? I'm not letting her do this again. It's my fault she—"

"Do what, Rhett? You're not making any sense."

"Come on, Mr. Farris."

Rhett straightened and with a strength the EMTs were not braced for, he shrugged them off.

"Wait! Louise, please. Where is she? Where did she go this time?"

Confused empathy, so soft, graced her face. Rhett wanted to beg forgiveness for frightening her.

She took both his hands. "She called me a few hours ago. She said she was going to spend the night at her house."

"House? What house?"

"The one she inherited. She didn't leave you, Rhett. Here." Quickly, she turned and scrawled across an envelope of junk mail. "This is the address. Go see her yourself."

Authority grabbed him under the arms.

"After we make sure you're not going be a danger driving, Mr. Farris."

BIRDS DRAWN IN SOFT lines stared at vistas unseen in their still life world. Drifting in and out of exhausted dozing, feeling herself dry of tears, Cassandra wondered what the artist imagined the birds were seeing. People in the distance, their lives unfettered in a watercolor world? Water rippling on a lake, touched into motion by a fallen leaf. Maybe they watched other birds, and the artist captured them before they took flight, disappearing in the fluid motions of a flock.

Part of her wished she could fly away, too. Just high enough to be free of the hurt and comprehend without emotion clouding her sight.

She should have seen it, even back then, should have sensed something was off. Yet, her head was so far up her own backside, so focused on her wants and needs, she spared no thought for why Rhett felt the way he did.

Truly why. Not the reason he gave her.

Laying on the sofa, Cassandra wanted to excuse herself. She'd been nineteen. What does anyone know at nineteen? Arguably, not much. However, this was the man she wanted to age beside, and she knew his body hummed for her. She should have been smarter.

Although Rhett had not known, either.

Against the look on his face haunting her, she shut her eyes and turned her head towards the wall. No man, who could rein in the world with his bare hands, should have to look so defeated and shamed. In the bedroom, she wanted to take him in her arms and do all in her power to soothe.

Right now, she wanted to grab him by the shoulders and shake him.

True, he'd be the one to deal with this more than she'd ever understand, but she should have looked past her own nose and recognized something was wrong. Imagine if she'd seen it sooner. They could have spent all the wasted years working on it. He might be free by now. Or at least, he wouldn't be at the beginning of such a trial.

What help looked like she didn't know. Nor did she know how much or little she ought to encourage he seek help. Sure, he was a man and stubborn, but Rhett was generally sensible. However, this *thing* wasn't connected to reason and men had gone to war over far less.

Cassandra opened her eyes. Doubtless there was a wealth of information online and she could even drive to the library and check out books. Rhett Farris wasn't a case study, though.

She didn't want to appeal to him from a researched point of view. She wanted to come to him as herself, loving him as she did.

Frighteningly, though, Cassandra had to admit Rhett might not want to come to her. Not after this. Whatever stayed in place, keeping him from becoming his father, might snap and he'd retreat into obstinate darkness.

Groaning, she sat forward. In getting all the furniture and her own things out of storage, she should have stocked the kitchen. Food didn't sound appetizing, but she wanted the distraction.

Unlocking the screen on her phone, she searched for the nearest pizzeria and ordered a small green pepper, garlic, and black olive cheese pie. Good for dinner and perfectly acceptable cold from the fridge for breakfast. She didn't want to go back to her aunt's; she wanted to start nestling into the house.

In coming back, with or without Rhett, she'd sworn to put roots down and now, everything in flux, seemed like a good time. She didn't have the tenderness of his embrace to distract her, nor the rich resonance of his voice warming her.

Not that she relished having time to unpack the stack of boxes lining the wall; however, the pizza would be awhile, and she did herself no good a blob on the sofa.

Using car keys to cut into the moving boxes, she tried to encourage herself. Busy hands and a busy mind deciding where all her things would go, might clear her mind to think of what she could say to Rhett.

Whether or not his proud ass admitted it, he needed a way to untangle himself from the mess that had woven around him for so long. And frankly, though she would get down on her knees if it helped him stand taller, Cassandra needed to be humble enough and recognize she could not heal him from this.

MORE THAN A HALF HOUR later, elbows deep into a box full of clothes she didn't remember packing, hangers were nowhere to be found, a swift knock rapped on the door.

"Coming!"

Leaving said items in a jumbled heap, she grabbed her wallet and moved to answer before the door she'd forgotten to lock swung inwards and Rhett stepped through.

He looked terrible. A bandage over one eyebrow with a bruise bleeding outward, his skin was devoid of all the ruddiness sun and wind had given him. Perhaps worse, he looked at her like an animal desperate to trust.

The hurt and hope in his eyes struck her like an ultimatum and every muscle contacted to rush him and bring his body to hers. However, she knew better and turned her hands over, exposing her palms, like she'd done many times with spooked horses. No tricks. No sudden motions. Everything is visible.

"I hope you don't mind," he began. "Louise gave me the address."

Of course, I don't mind, you idiot! What in Heaven's Name happened to you? What happened after I left the house, Rhett? I didn't want to go. You should have let me stay. Even if we sat on separate ends of the room, I would have respected anything you wanted. You should have let me stay.

"I'm glad she did."

Why did you go and see her, though? Don't you have my number? You have my number. You should have called me. Wherever you were, I would have come. Don't you know that?

He reached for the back of his neck. "I thought you'd be there."

"I gotta get moved in here, eventually."

"I thought," he stammered, rocking weight between both legs. "I thought..." His voice cracked. "I thought you left. Again."

She stepped towards him. "No. Why would I leave?"

He coughed and tried to steady his tone. "Well, it wouldn't be the first time."

"I'm not going anywhere, Rhett."

"Why not?"

Reason told her to stay still, but the strain in his tone and expression pulled her beyond her strength. Towards him she moved, but he caught her shoulders, his arms straight.

"Ass! Because I love you, that's why!"

His grip tightened.

"Love me, huh? Is this the kind of man you want to love? A shit show who can't get it up to—"

"Don't!" She covered his mouth. "Don't say that. You're not the kind of man, you *are* the man I love. Are you going to accept that or not?"

He pushed her from his hands.

"I accept it. But are you gonna accept a man who can't fuck you because his father fucked him up in the head?"

She didn't answer. What kind of answer was there to give?

Rhett paced around the room, both hands behind his neck. He moved like a caged animal who sees the gate has been swung back on its hinges but distrusts the seeming liberty. If she tried to lead him out, he might rear back, teeth bared, and ready to defend what he'd been fighting for so long.

It hurt.

She wrapped her arms around herself to keep from trying to guess what he wanted to say. For as long as she'd known him, it was impossible to anticipate how a person reacts when their view of their own life crashes down. Everything Rhett considered and relied on within himself had been chucked against the wind. In the absent wake, he'd been left stripped bare. Platitudes of "it's okay" or "everything will be fine" teetered on insult. Like a bandage over a cut artery.

Turned towards the window and away from her, he stopped.

"All my life, I had *him* standing over me. Tom wasn't built for his family ranch dynasty, and I betrayed him just by looking him in the eye. I couldn't live under his regime and let him be right." Rhett paused. "I cut myself off from him. Had to. And," he cleared his throat, "it stung to watch him play daddy with you. But if there was going to be a way for you to be happy in our life together, then that was fine."

From the window, he turned around and leaned on the wall. In the ensuing pause, she inched towards him.

"I though I was right, Cassandra. I thought I was going to do everything right and we'd start this perfect life on the ranch together. You were," again, he cleared his throat, "perfect. And everything was going to be perfect, and I thought I could make it so." He looked at her. "I'm sorry. I'm sorry I tried to engineer our relationship."

Harder, Cassandra dug her nails into her sides to keep tears from welling over.

"I guess," he continued, "I had to have control because...I damn for sure can't control one thing."

Smarting heat burned her throat. Drawn to the dull, defeated, hazel eyes, she moved. "I was wrong, too. Young, stupid, and selfish. I couldn't see you because all I could see was what I wanted."

The doorbell rang.

Impatient and her vision starting to betray her, she grabbed a fistful of dollars before flinging open the door and shoving it at the delivery boy. The cardboard box, warm and emitting wonderful aromas she couldn't stand at the moment, got tossed onto the kitchen counter.

"I don't want your lunch to get cold on account of me."

"Don't play the hero."

"About all I have left, isn't it?"

"What's that mean?"

"I'm not asking you to stay tied to me, Cassandra. I don't know how to fix this, Who knows how long it would be before—"

"Who cares?!"

"Me!"

He pushed off the wall and strode towards her.

"I want to know I can take you in my arms and kiss you 'til we both tumble in that bed, and I lose myself in you. I want every moment of being in you."

"They're yours!"

She grabbed his hands and pulled his arms around her own waist. Against her breasts, she felt his chest heave and combed her fingers through his thick, dark hair.

"Those moments are yours, Rhett, because I give them to you."

He searched her face, her mouth, his gaze traveling lower down her neck until he dropped his forehead atop hers. Tighter his grip became, and she relished how it hurt to breathe in his arms.

"I'm an ass," he whispered.

"You're mine."

"Yes, ma'am."

She felt his lips press to her forehead, the bridge of her nose and then to her lips, seeking and deepening until they both lost themselves to one another entirely.

The end.

Thank You, Lord. For this chance and this gift. The teenager who sat huddled over a small journal, writing her heart out in coffee shops, at home in this one green chair, and in the cafeteria—she thought there was a magic key to publish a book. And it was one she'd never find.

Maybe there was and You handed it to her.

Also by Bree M. Lewandowski

August Nights
Under Midnight Lights: Part Two
Under Winter Lights: Part One
Chevalier
City of Kings
Constellations
Rogue
Heroe
This Delicate Thing
Shattered
76 Seconds
Midnight in the House of Lang
Adagio
Shelter
Me & Him
Unbroken Vow
Consequences to Our Planes of Existence
Saratoga Roan
Reverence of a Ronin